Ballads and Bedtime Stories

from

Michael Dustin Youree

Ballads and Bedtime Stories

Michael Dustin Youree

Cover art by Theraphosath

hardcover ISBN: 978-1-938505-54-6

Paperback ISBN: 978-1-938505-55-3

E-Book ISBN: 978-1-938505-56-0

Library of Congress Control Number: 2020949056

First Printing [Hardcover] ~ January 2021

10 9 8 7 6 5 4 3 2 1

Published by Lionheart Group Publishing, Colorado, USA

visit us on the web at www.lionheartgrouppublishing.com

Dedication

To those who keep me learning, chasing, and dreaming.
You know who you are.

Thank you for picking up this book.

I hope it brings joy, reflection, and adventure.

Ballads and Bedtime Stories

Table of Contents

Preface

I remember a particular Sunday morning in New York. It was Easter and I was headed to an audition. Having lived in the city almost three years, I confidently walked down 5th Avenue like a local.

This was my metropolis. I wasn't that Texas boy anymore. Or that Colorado college kid. I was still that dreamer, though, and as I stepped into a random, midtown tower off of Bryant Park, anything was possible.

The audition was for a documentary film set to follow the faith of a select group of New Yorkers. It wasn't a religious thing. More like an excavation of interesting human practices. The producers asked a single question: what is your philosophy on life? My answer was simple: I am a frog on the table, a rat in the lab, a monkey in the cage. Life is an experiment. We are meant to be dissected, tested, and shot into space.

Well, I didn't get the part. I'm not even sure if that documentary ever got made. Disappointments weren't uncommon. That's the life of an artist. Setbacks are like shadows. They're almost always there and you can't escape them. New York will chew you up and spit you out. Better learn how to take a punch or you will be down for the count. That's why they say, "If you can make it here, you can make it anywhere."

I carried on up 5th Avenue past the crowds at Saint Patrick's Cathedral. My typical melancholy mood had me grasping for something greater than myself. My wandering feet brought me to an inconspicuous side door in the hubbub of holiday Manhattan. It was open.

I went in to find an empty chapel. It had the flair of a Catholic institution but I wasn't sure as to its denomination. The Baptist churches I grew up in didn't have the ornate, gold trimmings or the little benches to help you kneel for long periods of time.

I found a place among the dead silence, closed my eyes, and bowed my head.

What comes next is lost in the myriad of memories like it. Many times, I've found myself in houses of the holy—from ashrams to oceans, exploring the nature of my humanity and craving a connection to the heavens.

Looking back on that moment and others like it, what resonates throughout is a devotion to that simple answer: we are all experiments in stardust. A true masterpiece is not a particular song or story. It is a life fully lived.

I spent nine years calling various neighborhoods of New York City home. Seven more, I couch-surfed around the world, embracing a nomadic life for the sake of my unquenchable curiosity and desire to expand my worldview. These stories and songs are treasures unearthed in the laughter and lesions.

- *Snoozing Suzy and the Stew* is a moment of whimsy through a broken heart left in Amsterdam.
- *Lullaby* is a loving embrace for my young niece and goddaughter across the distance between us.

- *Allegory of the Maze* is a pledge to live in the moment and appreciate beauty even in difficulty.
- *O Captain* is a reminder that the glory of living is not found in sitting lazily on the beach.
- *A Fable of Sun and Moon* is a wrestling match with infatuation found in a Spanish summer.
- *Forever Young* is the acknowledgment that we human beings never grow old in the context of an infinite universe.
- *Allegory of the Caveman* is my constant thirst for knowledge and grappling with all that I cannot understand.
- *O Captain* (Part 2) is a contemplation on the fears we find in dark, foreign places.
- And, finally, *Wily Johnny's Journey to Space* is a playful treatise on what it means to be an adventurer.

I call it *Ballads and Bedtime Stories*, a collection of song lyrics and short stories that you might keep on your nightstand.

Standing on the shoulders of giants like Aesop and Dr Seuss, I seek to shine a light *Where the Sidewalk Ends* and bring *The Velveteen Rabbit* to life.

With these poems and tales, I hope to inspire the Charlie and Alice in all of us, as we taste the chocolates of wonder. The golden ticket of life is already yours. These words are merely magic beans.

Gazing at the heavens, that dreamer in me whispers to the one in you: "Look for the Easter eggs."

Ballads and Bedtime Stories

Michael Dustin Youree

Lionheart Group Publishing
Printed in the USA

Snoozing Suzy and the Stew

Suzy was busy dreaming of stews,
The morning was calling but again she hit snooze,
Sleepyhead Suzy loved lamb shank and broth,
But every eight minutes, her alarm it went off.

Slowly and lazily she sat up in bed,
Into her computer her password typed in,
"Houpsyafloupsya" was her secret code,
The alarm stopped its howling and finally she rose.

Into the kitchen 'twas coffee she craved,
She needed espresso to waken the day,
The machine it roared its mechanical growl,
Her black and white kitty meowed on the prowl.

The milk it steamed, the coffee it dripped,
Puss was fed as her latte she sipped,
Two spoonfuls of sugar to Suzy's delight,
Her eyes now wide open, her spirit bright.

Still something had slipped Suzy's mind that day,
The window was open while outside it rained,
What fell from the sky was no typical pour,
It soaked her apartment with something much more.

A magical storm blew in from the sea,
It covered the floor while she brushed her teeth,
To the left and the right, above and below,
Her world was changing, though she did not know.

Over her toes the water it washed,
When Suzy looked down, she was totally shocked,
The water it rose with incredible speed,
Before she could blink it was up to her knees.

And so startled Suzy to the window ran,
By the time she arrived it was up to her chin,
It was then Suzy noticed the strangest thing,
The cause of the flood was her house was shrinking.

Now Suzy swam in an ocean of rain,
Her coffee and kitty small just the same,
Her table and chairs, her pots and pans, too,
All tiny like Suzy, bobbing 'bout the room.

But what stayed the same size was peculiar for sure,
It was all the fresh food from her vegetable drawer,
Giant onions, potatoes, spices, and herbs,
Now spun around Suzy as the water is stirred.

Then the thought struck as pepper passed by,
It all added up to a stew she could try,
Indeed, she was hungry and this her prime dish,
So miniature Suzy let the slurping commence.

Though the portion was massive to her tiny tummy,
Anything's possible and the taste was quite yummy,
Ate and she ate 'til she felt like exploding,
All the while she was growing and growing.

And so stuffed Suzy returned to right size,
The rain was now over, the sun filled her eyes,
Though she was drenched, her whole house a mess,
Suzy felt cozy cuddling Puss with a kiss.

As she started to doze distant sounds she could hear,
Louder and louder the song it drew near,
Then it hit, a howl so familiar,
Eight minutes were up, her slumber now over.

Lullaby

Here's a song,
It's just for you,
A thousand miles away,
I wrote this tune,
So I could sing to you inside your room.

Though I may be far away,
I think of you every single day,
So, rest,
And for you, I will play.

Close those little eyes for me,
I'm singing you to sleep,
Joyous dreams are yours, my sweet,
And I am yours to keep.

Days will come,
Days will go,
Times will change,
But always know I'm here,
To walk with you on life's open road.

Along the path, don't forget to laugh,
But when you cry, I'll hold a handkerchief,
And hand to help you up again.

Close those little eyes for me,
I'm singing you to sleep,
Joyous dreams are yours, my sweet,
And I am yours to keep.

Should the distance get you blue,
Hum along to this lullaby's tune,
May it warm your heart and easy your mind,
May my love for you be all you find.

When you close those little eyes for me,
And sail on into sleep,
I'm your captain on the open sea,
Together we'll chase our dreams.

Allegory of the Maze

Twin boys stood at the entrance to a maze. Identical in appearance, there was little to tell them apart but for a particular character trait.

The first boy was sure of himself, confident to enter the maze and focused on a goal: to find his way through and claim whatever prize lay on the other side. The second boy was less confident. Willing though he was, he was unsure about the maze and what could be gained.

His brother assured him a great treasure awaited in the end, and that was reason for excitement. Reluctantly, the unsure boy followed his brother into the maze, for there was nowhere else to go.

The maze twisted and turned over green, tree- covered hills and through barren desert valleys, across bridges that swung over the clouds and into caves so dark the boys couldn't see their feet. A long way they walked.

They eventually came to an open meadow. At its center sat a crystal lake. They raced to the shoreline and peered into water so still it was like glass. In its reflection they discovered they were no longer boys, but young men.

In the distance, on the opposite bank, they noticed a large tent poking at the sky like a crown. They hurried to it. With each step the smells of garlic and butter, cinnamon and clove filled their noses. Their stomachs growled like hungry lions.

Inside they found tables that stretched as far as their eyes could see, upon which was a massive spread of ornate dishes piled high with food. There were cured meats and cutlets, fruits of all flavors, stinky cheeses, crumbly cheeses, warm breads, candy-coated pastries, nuts and dates, cakes and cookies.

The unsure young man was dazzled by the feast at his fingertips and reached out to capture a taste. But his brother stopped him with alarm.

"Wait!" he said. "This is just a trick to keep us from reaching the end of the maze."

The unsure young man stared back at his brother, conflicted. His mind mulled over the confident warning of his companion versus the tickle of his taste buds.

After a moment, the unsure young man told his brother, "Go on."

Perplexed, his brother asked, "But don't you want to claim your treasure?"

"Well, yes, but I am hungry," replied the unsure young man simply.

His brother wasn't going to waste time with such petty needs. He moved on, leaving his twin behind.

The unsure young man ate, stuffing his face with all the deliciousness before him. He devoured ham and brie, mango and honey, salted cashews and coconut cream. He became full but could not stop. He ate and ate until the glorious feast no longer made him salivate.

Instead, his stomach ached. He could hardly move. He threw himself down upon the soft, grassy sands of the crystal lake.

For a time he rested there, periodically returning to the tent to try something new, until one day he was ready to continue through the maze. He stuffed two of his favorite sweets into his bag and traveled on.

The maze continued through a dim-lit canopy of trees, up over rocky boulder fields where plants no longer grew, down snowy landslides, and across a mist-covered marshland, until the unsure young man found himself lost in a dense fog.

Though he could not see further than a few footsteps, he felt the hair on his head reaching down, tangling with his now long, thick beard. He knew he was a grown man.

Just as that realization hit him, the fog dispersed and a grand golden gate appeared before him—beyond which was a fascination he had never before seen.

In view sat a vast city with towers that shot into the clouds, and lights that flashed in colors he'd not yet encountered. People rushed from place to place at a pace hard to fathom. Flying machines and fashions unseen filled his gaze.

At the gate stood a keeper. He noticed the grown man.

"You again," said the keeper.

The grown man was confused.

“Me again?” he asked, “I don’t believe we have ever met.”

“Ah, you are correct!” replied the keeper. “There was one who came by before you. He was identical, but I can now see that there is something different about you.”

The grown man knew his brother must have passed that way.

“Come in,” coaxed the keeper, opening the gate wide. “Your twin refused to enter, but this city has much to offer!”

With little hesitation, the grown man stepped inside.

In the massive city of wide streets and hidden alleyways, of honking horns and endless chatter, the grown man was introduced to an entirely new world.

He cut his hair and shaved his beard in exchange for a necktie, fitted suit, and pair of shiny shoes.

He learned how to haggle for goods, barter in markets, and deal in coins, gold, and silver. He became aware of ambition—rising higher in the skyscrapers with each new talent, financial gain, and political connection.

He became quite popular in social circles for his skill at capturing moments on camera, and a wit to match it. At wild parties, he met space travelers and entertainers, presidents, and prominent personalities. He learned of wine and women, power and its pitfalls.

In time, it became tiresome. Just as the tallest towers have their tops, so, too, does opulence have limits. He packed his travel bag, pocketed his favorite pictures, and carried on down the maze.

He passed over endless desert dunes where the wind whipped and weathered his skin—the flying sand even tearing at his once fancy clothes. In his thirst, he longed for the endless pour of past parties. In his hunger, he longed for the days by the crystal lake. He contemplated turning back, but the distant trickle of water dripped into his mind like a mirage.

He could hear it. Was it real?

The sand turned to rock and the dunes gave way to a narrow, deep canyon. Down he climbed, out of the blistering sun and into the shadows where, at last, he found a stream. After refreshing his parched lips, he followed the growing rush of water until he came to a great sea that stretched beyond the horizon. On its shore sat a small, wooden boat.

Without hesitation, he climbed aboard and paddled. The wind returned, filling his sail and propelling the little vessel into the blue. Many days and nights he spent on the open ocean. Only afternoon rains provided an escape from the monotony.

In his boredom, he noticed his hands had become hard and calloused. As many moons past, he peered over the edge at his reflection. His hair had turned silver and deep lines ran around his eyes. He was a mature man.

At last, he caught sight of a tropical island. As he drew closer, he heard someone singing. A harp accompanied the sweet sound. He navigated closer and saw a beautiful woman. He brought the boat ashore and caught her eye. She continued to play as he approached her.

“You have returned,” she said.

"No," the mature man replied, "but you may have met my brother."

"Yes," she said. "He never came ashore. I welcomed him but he cursed at me, calling me a siren, a distraction from his goal."

"I am not my brother," said the mature man with resolve.

She stopped playing and came close to him. The smell of lilac and lavender was intoxicating. She then took him by the hand and led just beyond the beach to a cozy hut where he was able to rest from his long journey.

On the solitude of the island oasis, the two passed time together. The mature man discovered peaceful comfort in conversation and her caretaking embrace. The clock was of no consequence. He entirely forgot about the maze. There was only the paradise of palm trees, perfect temperatures, and the pleasure of her perfume. She taught him how to swim and sing, to garden and weave. She taught him about love, and he cared for her more than anything life had put in his path.

Still, all things must pass. Bliss does not last. The maze worked its way back into his mind and he longed to carry on. He pleaded with the woman to come with him, but the island was her home.

She could not leave. He could not remain. Though it deeply pained him, he was compelled to sail again. As they said their goodbyes, she placed into his travel bag a small vial of her perfume. Carrying memories, sadness, and uncertainty, he journeyed on.

Storms kicked up as dark skies enveloped his vessel. Waves

battered his starboard and port. His bow and stern tilted and turned. The voyage was not unlike those of his past—long and far.

The salty, frigid sea drenched him, sending shivers through his body like he'd never known. Through the worst of it, he feared for his life. Death seemed only a drop away as he shoveled the flood from his sinking ship.

In the midst of his dilemma, the cold induced memories of warmer days and hunger became a delightful reminder of all that he had tasted. Loneliness transformed into a sobering serenity. Eventually, the tempest gave way to new land.

In the far reaches of the sprawling terrain, he saw the peak of a mountain, dusted in white. His body ached. Was the mountain his final destination?

Each step was more difficult than the last. His bones cracked, his body bruised from a life well-lived. But he was a strong man and steadily continued his assent to the snow-capped summit.

Up and up and up, through the pine trees and across the ice of frozen lakes, he climbed to a stone archway that drew him like a spring rose rises to the sun.

Beyond the ancient barrier, a barren field opened before him. He was suddenly overcome with the recollection of being a boy, standing with his brother at the entrance to the maze.

"This is the end," he thought, "I have reached it."

The only thing that occupied the pocket of tundra was a small cabin. A plume of smoke puffed from its chimney.

As fast as his old body could manage, he rushed to its door. When he reached the threshold, he paused, nervous and unsure of what might be inside. As such things have never stopped him before, he took a deep breath and entered.

It was a small place, bare except for one feature. There, in the center of the room sat his reflection. But it was no lake or ocean, no fancy city mirror. It was an old man he knew well, yet not at all. It was his twin brother.

"Hello again, brother," said the twin, a gruff bitterness in his voice. "This is the end, and there is no treasure. For years, I have searched this place beyond the archway but there is nothing. Many more years have I sat here wondering. Where have you been brother?"

The boy who became a young man, who had become a grown man, who became a mature man, and who was now an old man, told his story.

He told of the things he'd done and the places he'd seen. He let his brother eat the sweets he had saved.

He showed him the pictures he had taken and shared the smell of his love's perfume.

After hearing the tale, his brother looked at him, tears in his eyes, and said, "Dear brother, it is you who has found the treasure. It was not here, in the destination but along the path—along the journey that the treasure was to be found."

They sat together in silence until his brother fell into a deep sleep.

The content old man, once that unsure boy, stepped outside and stared into the sky. The stars, like a thousand eyes, lovingly looked down upon him. As he closed his eyes, the wind blew and whispered into his ears,

"Destination is an illusion. At every end, we begin again.

"Sleep now. A new journey awaits."

O Captain

Oh, Capitan, can you hear me?
I think I'm lost at sea
I got caught up in the island trees
And the song the siren sings
But breezes blowing o'er the ocean
Swept up and blew you away

Now these wide open sands are like desert land
What is beauty without company?
If you see my friends
Tell them set all sails to the wind
When the anchor's in you end up drowning

Oh, Polaris, guide us north evermore
For Poseidon beacons us to the ocean floor
And this storm it is the roaring
Raging rapids of the river Styx
And I can see the shore
But I will leave no man overboard

What ho, Hades, I can hear you
Will you kiss me goodnight?
This may be paradise
But all that changes is the tides
Too late I've found there's more than pleasure's device
I am deaf from lack of conversation
Blind from nothing new to see
Once I roamed the seas of uncertainties
Oh, what irony that now this island swallows me
If you see my mates
Tell them meet me where Cerberus waits
Open the gates
I'm going swimming

Oh, Apollo, sing me a song of the sun
That my men and my mast may keep
Sturdy and strong
For the abyss it shan't persist
And this ship shall see the stars pour out
Along the starboard bow
And somehow we'll sail on
We'll sail on

A Fable of Sun and Moon

Sun awoke with a burning hunger, a sure purpose. He believed knowledge was found on the other side, and he chased the horizon with a courageous zeal and consistent faith in the fiction he made fact.

Earth sat at the center. As she felt Sun cross, a fire sprang forth. Fields and fauna blossomed in the certainty of a warm embrace. Day in and again she could count on him. Like a summer day, he always came.

Moon awoke, unsure of what shape she might take. Life cycles. She knew it. More in tune with her moods than the movement of time, Moon drifted from one end to the next like a secret bottle on the ocean--the unpredictable flow of eternal unknown.

Earth was an island. As the message of Moon washed on shore, magic and mermaids showed. Stars spoke curiosities and possibilities of where you go when dreaming. Night after night, she danced with the depths of intuition's imagination.

When Sun saw Moon, he felt his reflection. He knew what he was chasing—a companion. She was an equal celestial. Nothing mattered more than Moon and the pursuit of perceived perfection.

When Moon saw Sun, she glowed with heat. Never had she felt such connection to another being. Still, obligation was to her own direction, the freedom of waning and waxing. With so many seas and even more suns, Moon carried on in an orbit her own.

Earth stood in the balance, rising and resting through the serenade of Sun longing for Moon. By day she found righteousness, but darkness brought recklessness. With Sun, she moved mountains. With Moon, she howled spells with the wolves and witches of her spirit.

Seasons spiraled. Like a desert craves the waves, Sun stayed the course toward his wayward obsession. Moon grew wild like the secrets of whales and black holes, souls and their searching.

Eclipse came. Sun entered Moon and filler her with his light. The birds went silent. The breezes ceased. A glittering sky of daybreak and dawn shrouded Earth, the golden ring of Moon with Sun at her back.

The moment passed and Moon moved on. Sun could not stop running, but now Moon was fleeing. The more Sun tried to reason her absence, the more confused he became. His flame went cold like a glaciered volcano, boiling underneath but sheathed in frost.

Moon meandered in the balance of her breath. The eclipse was bliss, but the fire needed missing. Earth was in winter and Moon stayed with her. Northern lights fell, the tears of Sun. Earth and Moon spun with the shadow puppets and planets, spring sleeping in their womb.

Sun watched from a distance. He noticed the presence of comets and creatures in the deep. He met Saturn and Jupiter. They too had moons who bore his reflection. Upon it they relied. Warmth returned as he let go of Moon on Earth, accepting the imperfection of their connection.

Moon became a mother of beasts and human beings, all born from the bounty of Earth's balanced bosom. From the comfort of their caretaker, they bowed to mystic Moon. Now constant in her movement, she curved like currents of water, feeding folklore and farmer in a drink from her river.

Sun was the center, a constant explosion and eruption beyond reason, the burning in his belly a bounty of energy for all. Dragon of his solar system, Sun no longer pursued Moon. He held his place with peace. She would return. In instability's embrace, Sun's companions paced in circumambulate procession.

Moon was a goddess, master of transitions and tides, the revolution that binds, the unknown that lies beneath and beyond. Earth was a daughter, Sun her anchor. No matter how the cycle spun, Moon felt Sun's light and transformed it into life.

Forever Young

Stranger, you know me,
I've seen you here before,
On this pathway to the sea,
Like rivers we're running on lonely mountaintops.
This ocean breeze,
It's calling all of us,
Through its whispers in the wind,
I can hear it asking:

Do you dream when you're wide awake?
Suns may set, but children we'll stay,
And these open skies will heal our wicked ways,
Forever young in these eternal waves.

Finally, we reach the sea,
Abundant together we are no limits,
Not scarcity,
We are possibility,

And I can't see the end.
All I see is stars in the heavens overhead,
They reflect down on me,
I can hear them asking:

Do you dream when you're wide awake?
Clouds descend, but still we radiate,
Sweet infinity is not so far away,
Forever young in this outer space.

Allegory of the Caveman

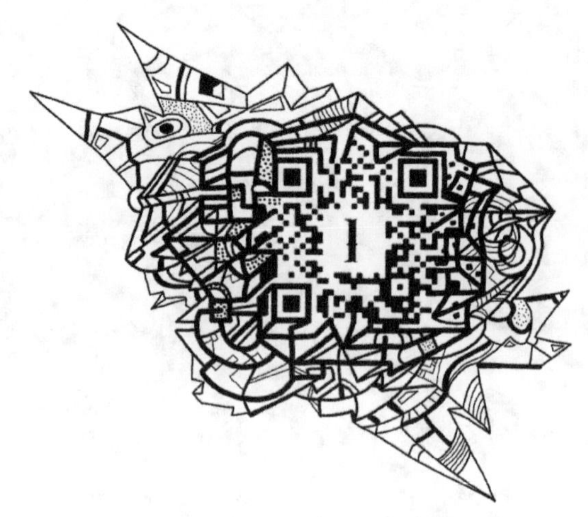

A caveman lived alone inside a mountain. He knew only the dark. Though just a boy, he had spent his entire life inside the cave. Only the smallest amount of light penetrated the depths of his abode, bouncing around his black crystal surroundings—just enough for his sensitive eyes to handle.

His time was spent hunting down the faint rays that found their way to him. He knew of no other world and convinced himself light beams were living creatures, very different but similar to his only companions inside the cave, the bats.

"Too fast for me are these white bats," he said to himself.

The more he chased them, the more he became obsessed with catching one.

Once, a particularly strong light beam hit him directly in the eye. It hurt! He was briefly blinded. After that incident, his relationship with the light turned sour. He believed he was at war with the white bats, for they wished him harm.

One day, while in combat with his white nemesis, he found his way to a massive overhead opening. Though it was no bigger than the size of a fist, it showered more light than he had ever seen.

He could not look directly at it. Turning his head away with his eyes hardly open, he walked cautiously toward the beam.

“What is this?” he wondered. “King of the white bats?”

He studied its movements and kept a safe distance.

Before long, he no longer squinted. He saw well enough that the beam wasn’t moving at all. It stood still, pouring from above.

It baffled him.

“You don’t want to be my enemy?” he called out to the white bat king.

Courage swelled as he approached. Eventually, he was close enough to reach out and touch the light. To his surprise, it did not hurt. To the contrary, it felt pleasing and warm.

His eyes traced the beam up to its source high above.

First glimpse of the opening sent a familiar pain through his eyes. He instinctively backed away but then he remembered the experience of squinting. So, he tried looking up again, keeping his eyes only slightly open. Sure enough, the light did not hurt.

He made a new home in that part of the cave and, in time, could study the skylight with his eyes fully open. Everything he had known to be true was not so. The light was not like a bat at all. It was a different kind of creature.

Counter to his previously held belief, it was a friend to him. Under the light, he was able to see that some rocks could be used to make designs on the cave walls.

His most fascinating discovery was rubbing two rocks together to make something similar to light. He ventured deep into the cave and watched the spark ignite the dark for an instant.

It was magic, as far as he could comprehend. And the skylight, a being who bestowed the gift. He drew pictures of his interactions with it. He worshipped it and often talked to it, hoping for a response. But it remained silent.

He grew frustrated.

"Why don't you ever speak?" he yelled up at the skylight.

Patience exhausted, he concluded it either could not talk or could not hear him. So, he decided to build a mountain of rocks that would allow him to get closer to where the creature lived atop the cavernous space.

Through backbreaking toil, he built a mound of boulders a quarter of the way up, climbed to the top, and called out.

"Hello?"

No response.

He built the mound halfway up and tried again.

Still nothing.

It was discouraging, but there was a curious development. The closer he got to the light, the bigger it grew. He had to build higher.

The pile of rocks was finally so high he could have reached out and touched the creature. That made him nervous. The creature had grown large enough to swallow him whole.

Will it hurt me? he wondered. *Will it punish me for coming too close?*

With clenched teeth, he reached out. Much to his bewilderment, there wasn't a creature. Instead he found a hole. His hand went directly through the light to a world beyond it.

It was a stunning discovery.

Confused and inspired, he decided to wait atop the rocks until the bright yellow light changed to the faint blue it always did. He'd made a mark for each time the creature went to sleep and there were now enough to cover the cave wall.

As he waited, sounds he had never heard before came from beyond the hole. It further perplexed him and stirred curiosity.

The faint blue finally arrived.

Again, he reached out, finding a ledge inside the opening. He tightly grabbed it, giving a tug to make sure his grip was firm. Taking a deep breath, he leapt from the giant boulder mound so the other hand could grab onto the ledge.

He lifted himself into a long, rocky column that reached upward through the dim light. Up he went, until his head poked out into an expanse of new wonder.

* * *

The caveman pulled himself out of the cave. Cautious and unsure of what lurked in the new place, he slowly rose to his feet. His heart raced. Giant beasts surrounded him—though they didn't seem to take notice, standing still as stones.

He walked. The ground was soft. He laid down in the darkness so he could stare up at the freckled sky of light hanging overhead. His greatest fascination—the giant ball of bluish white that seemed to rule over it all. Mesmerized, he admired the heavens.

He couldn't sleep. The sight of shooting stars, the movement of the moon, the rustling sounds all around, the shiver of cold down his spine kept him awake.

As day approached, he anticipated what would come, but nothing could prepare him for the glory of dawn. From the moment it touched the horizon to when the sun fully showed, he sat in motionless awe. Certainly, it was a God among Gods.

"What a magnificent creature you are," he grunted aloud.

The days and months that followed were spent acclimating to his surroundings. He learned trees weren't beasts at all, but quiet giants who spoke only when the wind blew. He made a bed of leaves and grass among them and spent much of his time peering out from their highest branches—always looking for a taller tree or what might lie beyond the forest. Maybe he could touch the beaming ball of light in the sky.

There was also an array of wildlife. The deer was his friend but the snake his enemy.

The most startling discovery came while trying his old magic trick. Striking stones, a leaf caught fire. It spread to other leaves, and eventually the branch. He tried to touch it, but its bite was far more fierce than the snake's.

With fearful fascination he watched as it grew, only disappearing as a heavy rain came. In the ash of destruction, he understood the dangerous power. He came to respect fire—careful in utilizing its necessary heat and light. He used the same stones always, as he was sure they were the conduits for magical power.

He lived a good life in the forest but wondered why there were no other creatures like him. The bats were numerous in the cave. In the forest, there were many animals, all of which had copies. The sudden awareness inspired loneliness and sent him searching.

He traveled far, but there were no signs of anyone like him. Reason led him to believe he was a god himself—alone like the light he worshiped. After all, he could harness fire, unlike any other living thing he had encountered.

Confident in that fact, he viewed himself as equal to the light.

Solitary though he was, he'd grown comfortable and forgot there were always more discoveries around the corner.

While drinking water at a nearby river, he heard an unfamiliar sound. Following it downstream, he saw the source of the sounds. What he found were three other beings like him, working. They wore strange coverings. He jumped into the brush in order not to be seen.

They move and look much like me, he thought. *But these creatures have fur of some kind.*

He watched, trying to understand what was happening. The creatures removed fish from the water and placed them into a large basket. The caveman had tried that before with little success. The beings had tools that made it look easy.

"What are they doing with the fish?" he asked himself. "And why are they keeping them from water?"

That was cruelty, he decided, and something should be done.

He crept up to the banks behind them where the fish were deposited—his stealth so honed the beings did not notice him rescuing the fish.

One by one, the caveman quietly returned the fish to the river until one fish wiggled free, slid out of his hands, and made a splash. That got the attention of the three beings.

For a moment, they and the caveman froze, startled and unsure what to do. Then, the chubby being pulled out a weapon and slowly approached.

"You, there!" he hollered. "What are you doing?"

The caveman could not understand their foreign speech. Fearful of their powerful tools, he backed away.

The stocky being calmly gestured to the chubby one—making him lower his weapon. Alternatively, the stocky being put his hands in the air. In his eyes, the caveman was more animal than human, and he deduced the caveman had no sinister intent. The stocky being whistled again, as they did while working, and gently moved toward the caveman.

The whistling sound was intoxicating to the caveman but that did not assuage his trepidation. Before the stocky being could get too close, the caveman grabbed the basket, hurled it at the stocky being, and darted into the woods.

The trio of fishermen chased after him. No matter how fast the caveman ran, he heard them close behind.

In an instant, he shot up a tree, taking refuge where he always had and thinking maybe they would lose track of him.

Unfortunately, that was not the case. The beings could not be fooled.

The Great Light in the sky is punishing me, the caveman thought in a panic. "I'm sorry Great Light! You are the most powerful. Forgive me for thinking I am your equal."

"Come down from there," called out the chubby fisherman.

"Can't you see he doesn't understand us," the stocky fisherman said, smacking the chubby fisherman on the arm. "You're only scaring him."

"There must be a way to get him down," said the gangly fisherman.

"What food do we have left?" asked the stocky fisherman of his companions.

"Good idea. I'll go and see what's in our knapsack," replied the gangly one.

He was back in minutes.

There was half of a fish sandwich and two pieces of fruit left. With his long arms, the gangly fisherman reached up and placed the food on a low branch, hoping to entice the half-animal, half-man from the tree.

The caveman cautiously watched their movements. When the

food was securely placed, all three fishermen disappeared from his view.

The caveman was smart enough to know a trick was afoot. He had done something similar before and was not going to fall for it. Instead of giving in, he waited.

Time passed. Dusk came and there was no sign of the fishermen. The savory and sweet aromas of the sandwich and fruit had long been tickling his senses.

Perhaps they are gone, he thought.

He slowly moved down the tree until the food was just out of reach. He snapped a small branch from the tree and used it to spear the food.

First was the fruit. He was familiar with its smell, for there were fruits all over the forest he had come to enjoy. He took a bite. It was good but not too different from other fruits he had tasted.

Tossing the fruit aside, he went after the sandwich. He inspected it. It was different. He took a bite.

Delicious! he couldn't help but think.

He devoured the scrumptious sandwich like a starved beast, licking his fingers when done.

The whistling again returned. Back on guard, the caveman froze. Out of the brush came the stocky fisherman, his hands out, exposing his palms.

The caveman was not alarmed. He understood the gesture to be one of non-violence. Then, he felt a little pinch. Investigating, he found a large splinter stuck in his thigh. Though he did not know it, one of the other fishermen had hit him with a poisonous dart. Almost immediately the sedative took over.

All went black for the caveman.

* * *

The caveman awoke with a jolt, finding himself in an unfamiliar place. It was like being back in the cave, except light poured in with orchestrated perfection.

Looking around, he saw the three fishermen. With them stood an odd-looking, tall individual with fur stranger than he had ever seen. It colorfully draped from his body.

The caveman timidly rose to his feet, feeling a bit woozy. The effects of the sedative had not fully worn off. The tall man with the strange fur approached.

The caveman tried to move away but the polished marble floors threw him off balance. He slipped and fell into the arms of the tall man.

"This is not fur," he discovered, feeling the fabric in his hands.

The tall, robed man allowed the caveman to investigate. Once the caveman was back on his feet, the tall man opened his robe, exposing his chest. He patted his chest and then patted the caveman's bare chest.

"I am like you," the tall man said.

The caveman did not understand the speech but the meaning was conveyed. He senses came back to him. The tall man signaled for him to look around.

The caveman found all kinds of objects made of trees and stones rubbed smooth. He found shiny objects and discovered translucent barriers which allowed the light to pour in.

When he looked out the window, his eyes were filled with a sight beyond his imagination.

A bustling village stood before him, full of beings and objects he had never seen.

* * *

The caveman went to live with the stocky fisherman and his wife. She made him clothes and taught him to speak their language. Every day he went to new places around the town. The meat markets shocked him at first. He had never thought of animals as food, though he did enjoy fish sandwiches.

He learned how to use their tools and marveled at their ability to control fire, water, and earth.

Music became an obsession. He listened to the stocky fisherman, an excellent whistler, and his wife, a gifted flute player, while pounding out beats on anything he could find.

In the mornings it was customary for every villager to sing the song of the sun. His adoration of the tradition was eclipsed only by time spent in the temple, a holy place in honor of the Great Light.

His relationship with the tall man grew from the beginning. The keeper of the temple was a spiritual guide, teaching him why the heavens moved and what it meant for beings the caveman learned were humans.

Once the caveman had a full grasp of their language, the tall man took him to the sea.

"This enormous body of water is a buffer between our world and theirs," he told the caveman.

"Who are we and what are they?" the caveman asked.

"They are gods and we are their children. Look," he said pointing to the horizon. "That is where our world ends and theirs begins."

The tall man went on to explain that long ago, Sun and Moon were the eyes of a singular being similar to them. In the time before humans, the being split itself in order to separate the evil from the good. The result was two Cyclops gods.

There was Sun, who represented all benevolent, and Moon, a representative of all malevolent desires. The blood spilt in the process created Earth, and humans grew like flowers from it. Thus, they were the children of the two deities, and the war between day and night a physical representation of the struggle inside them between right and wrong.

The tall man's teaching was that all must follow the way of the good Sun in hope of one day defeating the evil Moon.

"What about the other sparkles of light in the night sky? What are they?" asked the caveman.

"They are the souls of those who refuse the path of righteousness and are therefore condemned to eternity as prisoners of the night," replied the tall man.

"So, what happens to those who follow the path of righteousness?" further inquired the caveman.

"We join Father Sun. With each life the day becomes brighter, eventually winning the war and ending the night," said the tall man.

It made perfect sense to the caveman, for he felt the struggle inside himself. That day, he made a commitment he would follow the path of righteousness and reject the moon.

* * *

By spring, the caveman was fully acclimated to life in the village. It was time for him to become a contributor to its well-being. He was taken on as a farming apprentice and worked long, hard days in the field.

The village was a small, tight-knit community. Everyone knew everyone. Along with the stocky fisherman, the caveman made friends with young farmers who, like him, worked in the fields.

Often, they went to the tavern for pints of ale after long, hot days. The caveman favored a bartender—the saucy, skinny sister of one of his farmer friends. She liked that he was different from the others, and they soon spent time together alone.

Her hair smelled of sweet field flowers. The caveman thought he might one day make her his wife.

All was peaceful until one evening during the harvest, armored soldiers on horseback came riding. They approached him and his fellow farmers in the field.

"By order of the queen, this land and its resources are now the property of the empire," one horseman proclaimed loudly.

The horseman handed a formal proclamation to the caveman. It was signed and stamped by the queen.

"Give this to your leader," said the horseman firmly. "In two days' time, I will return to collect half of your harvest for the betterment of imperial territories, of which you are now included.

"Any attempts to undermine this process will be met with extreme prejudice and its conspirators subject to the full extent of the law."

The armored horsemen abruptly rode off, leaving no time for the farmers to question the soldier's actions.

The proclamation was immediately taken to the tall human. Distressed, he called a meeting of village leaders to discuss what should be done. The caveman insisted on being present. As courier of the proclamation, he was allowed.

A small gathering of prominent community members gathered in the temple. Though united in their anger, a unanimous plan of action could not be reached. Frustrated, the caveman spoke out.

"We must fight them! This harvest belongs to us!" he passionately yelled, quieting the room.

"My friend, we are no match for them," calmly stated one villager.

"They have a massive army and weapons of death. It will only bring us suffering and loss to fight them," said another.

"And do you fear death?" asked the caveman. "We must follow the path of righteousness and fight these infidels who seek to bring evil upon us. Even if death comes, we will join our Father Sun and win victory over the Moon. To do otherwise would serve as defeat and render all of us complicit in this darkness, condemning our souls to the eternal night."

The caveman's eloquent speech stirred the group. His faith touched their hearts, and they agreed with his assessment.

"Thank you, brother," the tall man said in a somber tone. "You have helped us see the higher calling in this. We will fight."

* * *

Two days later, the armored horsemen arrived with carts for carrying away the harvest. As they rode into the fields, impassioned villagers charged them with rudimentary weapons, mostly hunting and farming equipment.

The horsemen were caught off-guard at first, giving the villagers hope. But before long, reinforcements arrived to suppress the rebellion. As promised, it was met with brute force.

Violence unlike any the caveman had ever seen ensued. Not until he was a prisoner being carted away could he grasp the horror that had taken place.

The peaceful fields he had come to love were drenched in blood and covered with his friends' lifeless bodies. His teacher and mentor, the tall man, was among them. He had narrowly escaped death in the chaos and lamented he ever called them to action.

Deeply saddened, he looked up to Father Sun.

"Where is the good in this?" he hopelessly asked.

It was a long journey to the capitol city. Anger boiled as he sat in his cage. Over and over, the battle played in his head and he couldn't help but feel left behind by the dead and valiant villagers. They were with Father Sun.

He didn't understand. He was so happy in the little town. It had all been taken away. He was lost and alone, wondering if he would ever again see the girl he'd hoped to marry.

Before long, his wounds festered and ached. He wished for sleep. A bitter animosity toward the horsemen and the mysterious queen who sent them brewed inside him.

The prisoner convoy eventually came to an encampment. There he saw the imperial army's true might. Thousands of soldiers and machines of war sprawled across the open landscape.

Like a rabid animal, he was taken from his small cage and piled into a large vehicle with other prisoners. When the guards shut the doors, all went black. He was reminded of the cave.

When the doors opened again, he had no idea what time of day it was or how far they had traveled. In the sleepless span of darkness, he'd become delirious and disoriented. His belly ached with hunger and his throat, a desert crying for water. His body was weak.

Masked guards hurried the weary prisoners from the vehicle and dragged them to prison cells. The caveman could barely stand.

Doctors were sent in to attend the sick and wounded, of which the caveman was one. A gash in his leg had become so infected that he had a bad case of High Fever. The doctor's medicines saved his life, but they could not save his leg. It was amputated below the knee and replaced with a wooden peg. The brutal ordeal traumatized the caveman even further.

* * *

After two months' time, the caveman made a full recovery, though he still moved around slowly and required crutches.

He was not treated poorly but, in the eyes of imperial law, he was a criminal. It was made clear to him inciting rebellion was punishable by death. Soon, he would face the queen and her judges.

After another few weeks boiling in his cell and, thus, rediscovering his resolve, his day finally came.

As he stood in the courtroom, the caveman marveled at the grandiose architecture. It spoke of a modern world unfamiliar to him. There were two columns of statuesque guards on his left and right. Before him sat ten men and women cloaked in black.

They studied the caveman as he made his way—moving front and center. The judges rose to their feet. A woman dressed in fine clothing and glowing with trinkets entered, taking her place on an elevated throne behind the judges.

"Proceed," she announced.

The judges took their seats.

One remained standing and read aloud the charges against the caveman.

"You are hereby charged with sedition and violence against the queen's army, the penalty for which is death. How do you plead?"

The caveman did not understand the question. He stood defiantly silent.

"Well, go on, boy. What do you have to say for yourself?" asked the standing judge.

"What do I have to say?" he angrily retorted. "I have a lot to say. The offense here is not mine. I was peacefully minding the field when your queen's army forcefully came and stole what is rightfully ours. It is your queen who should be on trial. She is a thief."

The courtroom collectively gasped. The judges stirred. Never before had they been so affronted by a prisoner on trial for his life.

The queen, however, remained stoic, observing the situation.

"That is quite bold," said another judge, calming the room. "Our accounts show that force was used only in reaction to the uprising you and your fellow villagers instigated."

"What would you have us do, lie down like dogs while you steal our livelihood?" quickly responded the caveman. "I fought to protect food that belonged to us, not you, and I would do it again. What right do you have to take it from us? You are the criminals, not me."

The room exploded into a rabble.

"How dare you," said one judge.

"Hang him!" blasted another, receiving audible approval.

The standing judge pounded his fist on the bench in front of him, trying to regain order.

"Silence!" shouted the queen, as she rose to her feet.

The judges immediately ceased their banter. A tense silence came over the room. It was rare for the queen to speak out.

The queen stepped down from her perch and approached the caveman. Though he hated her, he could not help but feel a sense of awe as she came closer. Her majesty was impressive.

"Are you aware there has been a severe drought in the east, which is certain to be followed by famine?" she asked him.

The caveman did not respond.

"Are you even aware there is such a thing as the east or famine?" she continued.

He was not.

"I thought not," she said. "Well, you see, as ruler of this land, which is far bigger than your understanding, it is my duty to protect it from catastrophe. If this means taking from those who have plenty in order to save those who have none, so be it.

"It is unfortunate, but to carry out this task violence must, at times, be used. This is the way of the world. I do not expect your provincial mind to fully grasp this, nor do I require your endorsement. However, I will have you know that the confiscation of your village goods and imperial oversight of the territory was not theft, but charity."

The room again fell silent. The queen had asserted her dominance and authority. She turned to go, but the caveman stopped her.

"And what of your fine clothes and shiny jewels? What of your advanced weaponry and intellectual superiority? My village never had these things. Shall I take them...in the name of charity?"

"Those things are not required for survival," she said, turning back to face him.

"Easy for you to say. All my people are dead."

The queen had no quick response. She paused for a brief moment. "Carry on, judges," she said before leaving the room.

The head judge once again stood and announced, "You are hereby sentenced to hang by the neck until you are dead. The date of your execution will be determined in the coming days. Until that time, you will remain in your cell."

The caveman was promptly taken away and returned to the dungeon.

Late that night, the caveman was suddenly awakened by two guards. They quickly muzzled him and tied his arms. The caveman didn't fight back, submitting to their will. He was afraid but knew he could not alter his fate.

They took him down a long, torch-lit corridor at the end of which was a small door. They opened it, shoved him in, and closed the door behind him.

Still gagged and tied, he found himself at the base of a winding staircase—faint moonlight the only thing to guide him. Confused, he climbed the steps.

Up and up he went until he entered a small room. On the other side stood the queen. She no longer wore the decadent clothing and accoutrement of the courtroom. Her face was plain and her nightgown modest.

"I'm acquitting you on one condition," she said. "You must pledge to be my faithful servant and submit to imperial law. If you agree, you will stay here in the palace and train to be a knight and a member of my personal security team."

She removed the gag but left him tied.

"It is you and your law who have stolen my land and killed my friends. To pledge my life to you in order just to save it would condemn me to a fate far worse than death," the caveman said.

"What is that?" the queen asked.

"I would never be with my friends and Father Sun. I will spend eternity as a prisoner of the darkness."

"I want to show you something," said the queen with a softness in her voice.

She opened a hidden door behind her and directed the caveman up steps that lay just beyond.

He climbed the short staircase to a large room full of books and strange instruments. With only the moon for light, he saw strange silhouettes lurking in the shadows. One particularly odd feature stood out.

In the center of the room was a large contraption with an enormous scope that extended beyond the ceiling.

"What is that?" he asked.

She pointed to an eyehole. "Close one eye, and with the other, look through this."

He did as she directed but was bewildered with what he saw. "What is it?"

"What does it look like?"

"It looks like a pale desert. So dry it has lost its color."

"It's the surface of the moon."

He looked at her with disbelief. Now that she had his attention, she lit the room to reveal her laboratory—a space filled with observation equipment, astrological models, scribbled pages, and thousands of books piled on shelves and tables.

Struck with wonder, the caveman surveyed the room.

The queen continued to enlighten him on the virtues of science. She told him about the sun and the stars, and the solar systems around them. With her models, she showed him the movement of planets and explained the earth was actually round. She showed him her experiments on time and space and introduced him to the laws of physics.

"Everything I believed is a lie," he solemnly acquiesced. He remembered the experience of first leaving the cave. It was *déjà vu*.

"And this is just the beginning," she replied. "There is so much more I can show you, and even more I do not yet know."

"Why have you shown me this?" he asked.

"You have a courage and curiosity about you. You have shown the capacity to grow, even when it means the destruction of long-held beliefs. I need people like that, for knowledge like this is dangerous. It threatens the current social order.

"This room is still a secret to even some of the highest officials in my government. I want a peaceful transition from superstition to science, but I can't do that alone." She approached him, pulled out a knife, and cut his bonds. "So, I ask you again, will you join me?"

"None of this changes the fact that you ordered the massacre of my village. You talk of peace, but how can I believe that?" he asked.

"This is not an ideal world," she said. "There are limits on my power and compromises I must make to ensure my reign. Dishearteningly often, I am presented a scenario where there is no bloodless solution.

"I did not make the direct order to use violence on your people, but I did endorse the policy across the empire. Not only do I have a responsibility to protect those starving in the east, I must also maintain the image of authority. To do otherwise would undermine everything I'm working toward."

He didn't trust the queen, but he wanted to know more about all she had shown him.

"Very well. I will join you."

* * *

His training began the following day. Assigned to the naval division, his mornings consisted of low-ranking, laborious tasks such as cleaning and maintenance. The afternoons were spent studying politics, learning to be a seaman, and honing his combat skills.

Every evening, knights were required to attend a ceremony in worship of their order's deity, the God of War. It was his least favorite part of the day, but the caveman played along, as did the queen.

He looked forward to his evenings, which were spent immersed in the laboratory's books and maps.

His appetite for knowledge was insatiable. He devoured philosophy and literature, engineering and science. He read about different cultures and places he never knew existed.

As his reputation grew, he was invited to a secret meeting. Once a week, he, the queen, and a select group of knights shared thoughts, ideas, and discoveries.

The caveman came to love the queen and his fellowship of elite knights.

Several years passed. He became a learned sailor and thoughtful scholar. One night, as he was finishing up his studies, the queen made an unexpected visit.

“I have a mission for you,” she said.

“Anything you ask, my queen,” he replied.

“Five years ago, we began expeditions to a new land across the sea. One particular voyage was manned by knights loyal to me and led by a dear friend. When he returned, he spoke of a land more abundant than any he had ever seen, and that it was home to an ancient population. They possessed a mysterious knowledge he did not yet fully understand. He went so far as to ponder their origin as extraterrestrial. I sent him on a second voyage to investigate further but he has not returned nor sent word. All I have is this map.”

She handed him a tightly rolled canvas small enough to conceal in a closed hand. Once opened, it revealed a guide to a specific location just off a foreign shore. There were nautical directions the caveman understood and cryptic symbols he did not.

“In two days, another voyage leaves for the new lands. I want you to join the crew, find this place, and learn what became of my captain. You will have to do this in secret. These expeditions have become more about conquest than discovery. If this map and what I have told you fell into the wrong hands, it could be catastrophic to our understanding. It will be dangerous, and you will have to disguise your intent—perhaps even sabotage theirs but it must be done.”

“I understand,” said the caveman, committed to his duty.

As a parting gift, the queen gave the caveman a new leg. The wooden peg was replaced with the best prosthetic technology the queen had to offer. Engineered by her own hands, it was a token of appreciation and affection.

* * *

The fleet of five merchant ships set sail early in the morning with a crew of two hundred and seventy men. Dressed in full imperial uniform, the caveman was officially third in command under the captain and his first mate.

The caveman served as royal liaison for the voyage and it was generally accepted such an appointment indicated a formal endorsement from the queen.

The captain was a rough and rebellious sort with an obvious distrust of the queen's watchful eye. His distaste for the caveman's presence was clear from the start.

"You may have jurisdiction on land but the ocean is my territory," scowled the captain. "These are my ships and my crew. I will not have any interference. The merchants who financed this voyage have clear expectations and I intend to meet them, in spite of you."

"You will have no problems from me," the caveman calmly replied. "I serve at the pleasure of the queen, but you are the captain."

The longest span of time the caveman had spent at sea was three days and that was with a crew of his fellow knights. The captain's crew was a crew for hire. It would be a month before they expected to see land again.

Only a few days in, he was shocked by what he witnessed. In

the caveman's mind, the crew behaved like pirates. Their language was foul and their manner even more offensive. They drank heavily and frequently brawled.

The captain was the worst of them. His breath reeked of rum and his temper wildly volatile. One night he threw a man overboard for cheating at a game of cards.

For the most part, the caveman stayed separate, only presenting himself when he felt it appropriate to display feigned support for the voyage or to collect information regarding his secret mission. He often rested in the afternoon.

Late nights were spent deciphering the queen's map and plotting his manipulation of the merchant mission. It was the only time he was sure to go undetected.

Every evening the officers had dinner with the captain, where daily business was conducted and plans were made. At one of these meetings, the captain pointed his attention to the caveman, who usually remained silent and uninvolved in the proceedings, quietly consuming his dinner in hope of going unnoticed.

"Have a drink," the captain said to him.

"I'd rather not," replied the caveman.

"Pour this man a drink," shouted the captain to the sailor serving them.

"I said I would rather not."

"I don't care if you would rather not. I said you're having a drink, so a drink you will have," the captain snapped back. "You're enjoying my food. Now, you will enjoy my wine."

The caveman did not bother arguing. The sailor poured the wine.

"Drink," the captain forcefully said.

For a moment, the caveman resisted in his stillness, allowing a tense silence to come over the room. But he eventually took the glass. He knew it was better to give in than to cause further friction between the two of them—potentially jeopardizing his hidden agenda.

He downed the wine in one gulp, slammed the empty cup back on the table, and stared back at the captain.

A sinister smile came over the captain's face. "Pour him another."

As dinner continued, the captain made sure the caveman's glass was being emptied and then promptly refilled.

By the time they were done with the meeting, the caveman had consumed enough wine to make him drunk. Still, the caveman remained calm and quiet throughout. The captain dismissed the officers.

"You," he said to the caveman. "Stay."

The others left the room, leaving the caveman and the captain alone.

"What is it you do at night that requires you to sleep during the day?" the captain accusingly asked.

The caveman paused. He was caught. Wine was being used as a truth serum, but he would not let it blow his cover.

"Why does that concern you?" he asked, deflecting the question.

"Everything suspicious on my ship concerns me. Answer."

“I like to read, and the night is the most peaceful time to do so.”

“If you can’t read during the commotion of the day, then how is it possible that you sleep?”

“I have no trouble sleeping, as you obviously know. Why are you spying on me?”

The captain brazened a knife from his belt and violently speared it into the wooden table. “What are you hiding!?”

“I’m hiding the fact that I detest all of you,” the caveman snapped back, emboldened by the wine. “I’m just here to be the eyes of the queen and monitor the expedition. I don’t question you for your disgusting behavior. What gives you the right to question me?”

The captain grabbed the caveman’s collar and got in his face. “Answer me!”

Instinct and emotion took over. The caveman shoved the captain to the ground.

Enraged, the captain pounced back on his feet and flung himself at the caveman.

They furiously fought, punching and wrestling. During the melee, the caveman pulled the knife from the table and pointed it at the captain.

The captain unexpectedly laughed. “You see. You’re not so different from the rest of us,” he said, casually walking over to the cabinet for another drink. “Now, get out of here.”

The caveman was confused but he dropped the knife and walked to the door. Before he could leave, the captain spoke.

"I didn't throw that man overboard because he cheated at cards. That was staged for the crew." He held up a letter. "The man was consulting with pirates."

"Then why the show? Why not just tell the crew?"

"Because I don't think he's the only one."

"Why are you telling me?"

"I'm unsure about you, but a pirate you're not."

The caveman left the room and returned to his quarters. Bloodied and bruised though he was, the fight invigorated him.

He began to rethink his opinions. *The captain may be a brute but perhaps he isn't the ruthless madman I previously thought.*

* * *

Over the course of the next two weeks, the caveman was a familial part of the crew. Though he maintained a veil of deception, his perspective had changed.

He came to enjoy the rowdy nights of wine and the offbeat company of wily sailors. It brought back memories. Nights in the village tavern were not much different.

He remained focused on his mission and found the stories and conversations useful in unfolding the mystery.

They spoke of the new lands—how there were rivers running with gold. Of particular interest to him were accounts of native people. One sailor talked of a magical fountain of youth and claimed the native kings lived for thousands of years.

Another said they were so powerful they could control the clouds, the rain, the thunder, and lightning. Yet another called them children of the sun.

The caveman no longer believed in such superstition, but he felt they were clues on the path to unfolding the truth.

On occasion, the opportunity for one-on-one conversation occurred. He delicately asked about the queen's man, mixing his pointed inquiries with random questions on other subjects to throw the crew off any trail that he might have an ulterior motive.

He never received any definitive answers.

Most of them had heard of the royal crew and their captain, but stories of their whereabouts ranged from collective death to assimilation with the native peoples. In every case, the information led to more questions than answers.

To forget his frustration, the caveman lost himself in the stars.

Out on the open ocean, they were brighter and more plentiful than he had ever seen. He was fascinated with how the cartographers used the stars' consistent patterns as beacons in the vast, directionless expanse they sailed.

He melancholically reminisced of bygone days in the laboratory.

* * *

The weather had been kind to the voyagers but near the end of their journey, the wind died and a great stillness came over the fleet. Their particular ship was mired more than the others.

They were stuck—barely moving. It was a strange phenomenon, yet not unheard of.

Late one night, the caveman decided to take a walk on the deck. He expected to be alone but what he found was the captain leaning over the stern of the ship.

The caveman watched in secret. He couldn't work out what mysterious task was underway.

When finished, the captain returned to his cabin, unaware of the caveman's presence.

With the captain gone, the caveman further investigated.

Over the back of the ship, he found a thick rope attached and disappearing down into the water. He tugged on the rope, but it wouldn't budge.

He pulled with all his might. It took all his strength, but he finally revealed an anchor at the end of the line.

What is this? he wondered. *The captain is the one keeping the boat from moving...but why?*

He reset the anchor in its depths.

Baffled, the caveman couldn't figure what the captain was up to, but he knew there were more secrets than mutinous conspiracies.

At the officer's dinner meeting the following evening, the caveman was again asked to stay late. Once they were alone, the captain pulled a key out of his pocket.

"I have something for you," he said.

The caveman followed to the captain's private quarters, where the captain unlocked and opened a small desk drawer.

The caveman caught a quick glimpse inside, noticing a small, familiar device, but before he could get a better look, the captain shut the drawer and handed him a sealed envelope.

"What is this?" asked the caveman, taking the envelope.

"As I thought, the thief I threw overboard isn't alone. There is a much bigger plot at hand. That envelope contains information the queen will find very valuable."

"Why this sudden allegiance to the queen?"

"You're dismissed," the captain said, ignoring the caveman's question.

The caveman put the envelope in his pocket and left the room.

He was curious about the letter but the familiar device in the drawer filled his thoughts. Then it struck him. It was a barometer. He had seen that very same instrument used by the queen to predict weather patterns.

The implications of the discovery were mind blowing. That technology didn't exist outside the queen's laboratory.

He's a knight? he wondered. *No...can't be.*

Hungry for more answers, he tore open the envelope. Inside was a plain piece of folded parchment. To the caveman's surprise, it was not a traditional letter. On the paper were not words but a long series of symbols. He studied them.

Like the barometer in the drawer, he found them familiar but couldn't figure out why. Surely, he didn't understand the code. Patterns stood out but he couldn't formulate any meaning.

The wind howled. Distant thunder rumbled. A storm was coming.

He heard the crew hustling around, preparing to catch the wind and move the ship along. The caveman stayed in his quarters as the boat rocked and swayed in the uneasy water. He was engrossed in the strange letter. Questions flooded his imagination.

Why is the captain sending coded messages to the queen? They must have a past. Does this captain know the queen's captain?

The storm picked up. Waves pounded the ship. The caveman heard men barking orders, as the boat violently shook to and fro. And then, BAM! A wave hit the ship's broadside and sent the caveman and his effects flying.

He was concerned. That was not like anything they had yet encountered in their long journey. The caveman collected himself and opened his cabin door to a wall of rain so heavy he could hardly see. He worked his way to the ship's deck—the onslaught steady.

The sky and the ocean flung water from every direction. The crew furiously worked to keep the ship from being crushed by the storm's intensity. Lightning struck all around like horrible heavenly fireworks.

He slowly made his way to the bow of the ship, where in the

distance an odd phenomenon occurred. The lightning seemed to strike in one consistent spot, over and over.

Another wave smashed. The caveman held on for dear life. Then, as if struck by lightning, he remembered where he had seen the strange code in the captain's letter.

It wasn't the code itself but the penmanship. It was the same as that on the map the queen had given him.

Wait a minute. His brain churned like the waters around him. *If the writing on the map is from the same hand then...this captain is the queen's captain!*

As quickly as he could, he navigated the chaos in search of the captain. It was coming together. He saw the subtle hints the captain had given him. The captain wanted him to know. Flashing the barometer was a clue.

Through the tempest, the caveman hunted the captain, but he was nowhere to be found.

"Where's the captain?" the caveman yelled to the first mate. But the first mate was far too busy saving the ship to concern himself with the caveman's question.

The caveman darted for the stern—nearly tossed overboard in his haste. The captain's anchor had been cut loose. And then he saw it. Just off to the side in the tumultuous sea, was the captain in a small boat.

He tried to get the captain's attention to no avail. There was only one option. Without much thought, the caveman dove overboard in the direction of the captain.

His actions caught the captain's eye. The caveman struggled to swim. Impressed by his bravery, the captain tied himself to his small, buoyant boat and jumped into the water to aid the caveman. It was a struggle, but the two eventually made it safely onto the small boat and braced for the storm's impact.

"What are you doing!?" yelled the caveman through the ferocious, whipping winds.

The captain ignored him, too concerned with rowing and navigating. Understanding the urgency, the caveman grabbed a second set of oars and joined the captain in rowing.

Before long, the fleet was no longer in view. They were alone upon the ocean.

Though the caveman was unsure where they were headed, he had full faith in the captain and a feeling that his questions would be answered.

* * *

They rowed to exhaustion, battling the wind, rain, and waves. Only after the storm subsided did the caveman realize how miraculous it was that the small boat had not been destroyed in the squall.

The captain, focused on the mission, removed a device from his bag and dropped part of it into the water.

"What is that?" asked the caveman.

"It's called sonar," the captain replied. "It detects movement with waves of sound."

The caveman had heard of it in laboratory conversations but had never seen it in practice.

"What are you trying to detect?"

"You'll see," said the captain.

After a few minutes of silence, the caveman came out with it. "You're a knight, aren't you?"

The captain did not answer. He was focused on his machinery.

"You're the queen's—"

"Shhhh!" interrupted the captain.

The waters were completely calm again. The clouds dissipated and intense sun rays shined down.

The two unlikely companions carried on in silence until finally the captain broke his focus and again searched through his bag. He pulled out another small tool and twisted it. It suddenly glowed red.

The caveman was baffled. He had never seen anything like it.

The captain promptly threw the tool into the water and watched it sink. He looked at the caveman with wild eyes.

"Almost there," he said. "Now we wait."

"What are we waiting for?"

The captain grinned. "The queen sent you looking for me, didn't she?"

"Yes," the caveman plainly stated.

"Well, you can tell her I found it."

"Found what?" The caveman could hardly contain his excited curiosity.

The boat suddenly quaked and the water rumbled. They stared into the abyss, anxiously waiting for whatever would happened next. Down in the depths, a dark figure rose. As it grew closer and closer, the men were able to grasp its enormous size.

The captain showed no signs of fear. That calmed the caveman as the behemoth approached.

Just a stone's throw away, a gigantic steel beast emerged.

"That's no living thing," said the caveman, filled with wonder and awe.

"It's a submarine," said the captain. "Now come on."

The captain rowed. The caveman joined him.

As they approached the underwater vessel, a woman stepped out onto the deck, waiting for them.

The caveman knew what a submarine was, in theory. He had fantasized about the possibility, but never thought he would see one in reality. Experiments with models had all failed.

Upon arrival, they climbed a ladder to the deck where the woman waited.

"Welcome," she said in a warm monotone. "Follow me."

She led them inside and down a spiral staircase. Memories of the first time he ascended to the queen's laboratory flooded the caveman—the feeling similar.

Behind them, the door shut—initiating a switch of light that dazzled both the caveman and the captain. An electronic universe came alive all around them.

They watched as their mysterious guide interacted with it, leading them down a hallway that looked nothing like the mechanical submarine belly they had envisioned.

The guide seemed like part of the underwater vessel, as if she was not entirely human. Her movements were deliberate and sharp.

With the wave of her hand, a small room opened in front of them.

“Please step in.”

They cautiously entered the room. Though it was only big enough for the two of them, it was plush and welcoming.

“Sit down. Relax. It’s a short journey.” The door automatically closed as she walked away.

They took a seat. It was very comfortable.

As they relaxed, the seats came to life and rotated to face the outer wall. A strap shot over their laps and snuggly pulled around them.

Their alarm was only momentary, as the wall in front of them cleared into crystal glass, captivating them and revealing the ocean depths on the other side.

They watched in amazement as the submarine sank. It grew dark, but they could somehow still see the movement of creatures beyond the glass.

“Do you know where we’re going?” asked the caveman, breaking the long silence.

“Only a few moments ago, I would have said yes,” answered the captain, “but this is where my understanding ends.”

As they descended into the abyss, the caveman recalled climbing out of the cave.

He reached out and touched the submarine’s wall. It was warm, unlike the outside water world that would freeze a man in a second.

Deeper and deeper the submarine went. Weirder and weirder the sea creatures became—fish with arms, strange animals that looked like kites in the wind, a giant squid with more legs than he could count.

The journey continued until, eventually, the ocean became so dark nothing could be seen beyond the translucent submarine walls. The two men were engulfed in pitch black until the wall in front of them opened from the bottom, allowing light to slowly creep inside their small cavity.

It hurt their eyes, for they had acclimated to the dark.

The caveman was awestruck. Even with his acquired knowledge and understanding, he found himself feeling like that clueless caveman squinting into the light.

The portal fully opened, and his eyes adjusted to the sight of three seated figures. The figures beamed with light. The sound of chimes dancing in the wind echoed all around. The room sparkled. Gold and silver ornaments crested with a thousand different colors of gems surrounded the three seated figures.

To their surprise, the caveman and the captain were no longer strapped to the chairs but standing on their feet. Their weathered and wet clothes were gone. Instead, they were wrapped in fleece and draped in silk finery.

Their bare feet melted into the floors of plush carpet. Walls of the finest limestone surrounded them and stretched to lofted ceilings made of stained glass.

At the feet of the figures was a small fountain of crystal blue water. It hypnotically churned counterclockwise.

Everything was fantastic, yet what confounded the caveman was the foreign world that swam around the room. Images and symbols flowed like fish moving through water.

The caveman had seen these symbols before, at least some of them. They were the same ones found on the captain's map.

"What do they mean?"

Before the captain could answer, the room flickered. It began slowly but increased in speed until nearly unbearable—the bright, opulent surroundings strobed back and forth with an unknown darkness.

The caveman and the captain covered their eyes.

Trapped inside his head, the caveman remembered his first encounter with the light. He focused on the chimes. Distant drums resounded. They approached like a suspicious stranger around the next corner—closer and closer until everything went silent.

He opened his eyes. They were back in uniforms and alone inside a steel cage lit by a single overhead light. No exit could be found.

"What is this? Are we prisoners?" asked the caveman.

"You think I know?" asked the captain.

"You're the expert."

"No. We're both novices here."

A bolt shot from the metal frame, spraying water into the enclosed space. The captain sprang into action. He immediately ripped off a piece of his sleeve and used it to plug the hole. Just as he did, another bolt came loose, and then another.

"Well, don't just stand there!" yelled the captain.

"What is this?" asked the caveman, afraid and confused. Then he saw a single sign on the wall. Again, it was one of the map symbols. A wave of peace washed over him.

"Move it, knight! Act now. Ask questions later," barked the captain.

The caveman joined the captain in his strategy. It wasn't working. As soon as one hole was plugged, two more burst open. The water quickly flowed in. The flood consistently crept up their legs.

"This isn't working," said the caveman.

The captain stopped. "You're right. How do we get out?"

"A way out?" asked the caveman. "Aren't we at the bottom of the ocean?"

“At this point I’m not inclined to do much thinking, just doing.”

“And what do you propose we do? Get crushed by a wall of water?”

The captain got in the caveman’s face. “Listen, we have no idea what’s on the other side of these walls any more than we have any idea how we got here. We’re lost in a world beyond our imaginations. So put your mind aside. The only task right now is to solve puzzles, one at a time.”

“Puzzles?” The caveman hadn’t thought of it that way.

“Your leg, does it detach?” asked the captain.

“Yes. It does. Why?”

“I know that metal. It’s very strong. I helped the queen forge it. We can use it as leverage to pry one of these loose panels open. Once we do, the hull will flood and we’ll swim our way out.”

“Alright,” the caveman agreed.

He detached his prosthetic leg and they went to work. The water reached their waists. The caveman removed the metal foot and wedged it between two panels. The captain used the rest of the leg to hammer the foot further and further into the crack. Water flowed in more furiously. They took turns pounding on the top side of the foot, using its leverage to widen the opening far enough to get the entire leg into the gap.

When they finally achieved that task, the water level was at their chins. They shoved the leg in place and pushed with all their might to create an opening large enough to swim through.

The water was over their heads and they were losing leverage.

"Let me try something," said the caveman, as they came up for air.

He took the leg out of the gap and pounded it on the opposite, bent side of the metal frame. The captain immediately caught on. The jolts pressured the bolts that kept the frame in place.

The captain grabbed onto the leg and added the force of his strength. Furiously, they smashed. It was working. Soon the bolts came loose, freeing the entire panel and allowed the men to escape. They hustled toward a surface they hoped was above.

Without his prosthetic leg attached, the caveman couldn't move very fast. The captain disappeared out of view ahead of him. The caveman's breath ran short. His lungs ached as he flapped his arms and kicked his one leg as hard as he could.

Still no sign of the surface, he had nothing left.

As water filled his lungs, fear was erased by a state of bliss in the emptiness that came with his surrender.

* * *

In the absolute silence were only three seated figures. The caveman did not seem to have a body or any form. He was only his consciousness.

He moved closer to the seated figures, but they did not change in shape or size. He moved to the left. In that perspective shift, he saw there was something else behind the figures. There were more than three. Their faces followed him. Their bodies multiplied.

He kept moving left until, once again, there were only three figures. As if a thousand miles away, chimes played their whimsical delight.

* * *

The caveman was ripped out the odd reality with a jolt—spewing water from his nose and mouth. Once he regained his composure, he noticed the captain kneeling by his side.

With a look of relief the captain said, "Welcome to the miracle."

"What do you mean?" the caveman asked, still coughing as he recovered.

"Take a look around."

The caveman felt the loose earth beneath his hands. At his feet was a small pool of water.

"This can't be," he said with a shock. "I have two feet!"

"It's your gift," said the captain.

"My what?"

The captain pointed to the circular enclosure that surrounded them. On its stone walls were etched three of the map's symbols. They repeated in a rotating pattern around a base of a sprawling library, extending beyond his vision. With it, a walkway spiraled upward.

"I don't know what these symbols mean, exactly..." The captain pointed to one in particular. "But this one means something like, 'a gift'."

"How do you know?" asked the caveman, rising comfortably on two feet for the first time since the rural village of the tall man.

"When I was among the native people of the new lands, they used these symbols to designate important ceremonies or significant situations. Any time an offering was made, they used that particular symbol. Sometimes it was paired with people. Sometimes not. When someone died or when babies were born that symbol dominated. It all seemed vague to me until I became the object of an offering ceremony.

"Upon my second departure from their lands, I was brought into the chief's private quarters. There sat the tribe elders in a circle. The chief lit a fire in the center and sat me down beside it. They chanted in unison as the blaze grew. It was hypnotizing. I became dizzy and drunk on the incantation and the heat and smoke that filled the enclosed room. As the intensity rose, they suddenly let out beast-like wails of women and men going mad. It lasted just a few seconds. And then all eyes fixated on me.

"In my altered state, I had not noticed the fire was extinguished—the only light in the room, a magic glow of an origin I could not determine.

"The chief approached me. He coated his hand in the thick, black ash piled on the floor and ran three sooted fingers down my face, from my forehead to my chin. The elders rose to their feet. My heart raced. Finally, a woman I had come to understand was the chief's wife stepped forward and presented me with a gift. Before I opened the box, the chief used his thumb to mark it with ash. This was the symbol he wrote." The captain again gestured to the etched symbol on the wall.

"What was in the box?" the caveman asked with great anticipation.

"A dagger with a handle of gold and a blade of diamond sheathed in leather. It was not decorative, except for one feature. This." The captain now gestured to a different symbol.

"So, what does it mean?"

"I don't know, though it has been my obsession since the moment I opened that box. It's why I never returned to the queen as she expected. It's why I took on the disguise. Something happened to me in that room and I've been trying to solve the riddle ever since." The captain paused, wild eyed with discovery. "I have searched and searched for clues to this symbol's meaning. This is the first time I've seen it anywhere other than on the dagger."

The captain reached behind his back and revealed the sparkling trinket of violence. At the top of its golden hilt the caveman saw a symbol that matched one on the wall.

"What about this third symbol?" asked the caveman.

"It's the one I've seen the most. It's everywhere and part of everything for the tribal people. Most of them have it tattooed on their bodies. I've even heard them refer to it as something called 'Yedá'."

"But what does it mean?"

"I think we're getting closer to finding out. It's time you put that new leg to use. Let's go."

The caveman and the captain ascended the spiral. Moving quickly past rows upon rows of books written in languages they did not understand. They observed with unintelligible fascination. All they could deduce was that the languages were evolving.

It's like the passage of time, thought the caveman.

As they raced upward, the writing on the books' covers became more and more recognizable. Their paces slowed.

"This I know!" the captain said, abruptly stopping. "It's an old text the queen and I studied when we were children. It inspired our foray into the world of science but was eventually banned due to the highly controversial evidence that the world is much bigger than we previously imagined." He shook his head. "Fools."

The higher the two went, the more they found recognizable books. The captain proved to be very learnéd, and shared stories of he and the young queen—how they connected over the great novels of their time, admired the developments in thought, and marveled at the discovery of other worlds. They were the books that shaped their lives.

The caveman found a few. The first book he ever read was there, one once given to him by a tall man. He remembered its proverbs to the father sun. Some were committed to memory.

He scoffed. That was once his truth. Now, such faith seemed foolish.

"It has its own poetry," remarked the captain.

Just as it occurred before, but in reverse, the language morphed into an incoherent puzzle. Before they lost all concept of understanding, the caveman's eye caught something he knew. He ripped it off the shelf.

Upon the spine was the mysterious third symbol. He tore open the book. The captain looked on with equal anticipation. The caveman flipped through the pages until he found a picture. The men met eyes in shock. There was no question—it was their queen.

The captain grabbed the book and shoved it into his pouch.

"What are you doing!?"

"We're taking this with us," replied the captain.

"No. We should put it back. There's something holy about this place. It's a great collection of time and knowledge. We should not disrupt it."

The captain didn't share his reverence.

"The book comes with us."

The caveman reluctantly followed the captain until they came to a long corridor. The light changed and sound shifted. Beyond, they heard the chatter of voices.

The first corridor led to another corridor, from which many other pathways emerged.

They followed the sound—sprinting toward its growing vibration. The light became blinding. Their eyes were accustomed to darker places.

They finally emerged into a grand hall of chandeliers and tapestries. As their eyes adjusted, they found themselves standing in front of a crowd of people.

Though finely dressed, the galley appeared like a dying rainbow. To one side was a collection of off-white and mildly colorful clothing with a few spots of ostentation and boldness. It faded into the opposite side, which was covered in an attire so white it made the captain and the caveman squint more.

Finally able to see properly, they realized the chatter had turned into a room of gasps, and every eye was upon them.

* * *

They shared the stage with a figure in a flowing gown. It was covered from its face to its feet.

The caveman had read about ghosts. It was the closest thing he had seen to such a thing. It slowly moved away from them.

The room felt hostile. They had an inclination to run, but the captain and the caveman were surrounded and overwhelmingly outnumbered.

A bold one spoke. “Is this not exactly as we have been telling you?” Their voice echoed through the chamber, causing a stir.

“Constrain your ego and superstition,” grumbled one of the whites.

“Hear, hear!” flowed a few constituents. Hisses came from the more colorful side. The rabble escalated.

“Calm yourselves!” interrupted a woman in an off-white tunic.

Around her neck wrapped a blue ribbon with a small, red medallion. The room hushed. She gestured to the stage. "It's clear we do not know all there is to know."

Hisses came from the white side.

"Let the woman speak!" hollered someone in the mildly colorful crowd.

More hissing. Tension returned. Various factions shouted at the other.

The captain seized the moment of unrest to make his move. He unsheathed his dagger and thrust it into the marble floor beneath him. It sent a shockwave throughout the great hall—shattering the chandeliers and windows.

The diamond blade ripped the marble floor. Like an earthquake, a long, deep crevasse split the earth straight through the middle of the congress.

Some ran for their lives. Others shouted proclamations of doom. The captain and the caveman made a run for it.

A small band of whites noticed their flight.

"After them! We cannot let them into the streets!" the leader of zealots commanded.

In the confusion and riot, the second bold member of the house cried out in a furry, "Send in the guard!"

The captain and the caveman made haste down a lofted hallway of arcades. It was immaculately clean. Everything seemed in its perfect place, and the architecture pushed the boundaries of geometry.

"That's quite a trick you've got," said the caveman.

"I did figure some things out about this blade," smirked the captain.

They turned a corner to see the ghost-like figure standing in their path.

"This way," it whispered to them, and then disappeared into a hidden door.

The caveman followed without hesitation, moved by faith. The captain cautiously entered behind.

They exited into a courtyard. The dense garden was surrounded by four high walls and covered in a glass ceiling, much like a greenhouse. Amidst the overflowing flora lurked the ghost.

The captain and the caveman approached.

"Fear not," said the ghost, removing the flowing headpiece and revealing a human face. "I am not your enemy."

The human was no stranger to the caveman. The caveman knew the face and voice well—the human had been unconditionally kind and unwittingly deceptive. The caveman came out of the darkness because of him, and nearly died beside him.

How could this be? thought the baffled caveman. Before him stood the tall man.

"It's gotten out of control," said the tall man. "She's right. You are proof of our misunderstanding."

He went on to explain that his party of white had built a society on the belief that all knowledge necessary for human prosperity and happiness was already available through the accumulated learnings of the past. One simply had to become the library's books, surrendering self to the collective consciousness stored within.

"But it's all gone wrong," he said with sadness. "In our search for purity, we have become a party who frowns upon anyone not wearing white."

The ground rumbled beneath their feet. The walls shook.

"Our time is up. We must go." The tall man pushed open another hidden door. They crawled through the portal and escaped out into the street.

* * *

An urban jungle of metal and glass sprawled out before them. They were not on the ground but high in the sky. The street cut, curved, and cornered in all directions—to the left and right, up and down, as well. The network of roads circulated through windowed, steel giants like veins through a body. People and flying objects flowed like cells in the blood of a monstrous machine. It was harmonic chaos to the captain and the caveman.

A clap of thunder rattled their chests. They saw the exterior of the library. Even to the caveman it seemed ancient. Its presence was completely out of place in the shiny megacity.

A blast came from the roof. The single tower at the library's center collapsed, rocketing debris of stone into the surrounding buildings and street. A cascade of flying boulders and shattered glass disrupted the harmony they previously knew.

"You must go!" shouted the tall man through the cacophony. "Take this. It will get you where you need to go." He thrust a scroll into the caveman's hand and ducked back into the portal.

"Wait! You can't go back in there!" the caveman said in a panic.

The tall man turned back, revealing two off-white cloaks. He dressed the fugitives.

"Go to the western market. They will find you. When they do, give them the scroll. Ask for Yedá."

The captain's eyes widened. He grabbed the tall man's collar. "Yedá!? What do you mean by Yedá?"

"Go and see for yourself. I'm not one for faith but I think we need it now. And don't lose this." The tall man patted the stolen book in his aggressor's pouch.

Surprised by the revelation of his larceny, the captain released the tall man, who immediately disappeared into the portal. Just as he did, the walls crumbled, forcing the captain and the caveman to retreat onto the bustling city streets with other living things fleeing the scene.

Looking back as he ran, the caveman was horrified at the destruction.

All that knowledge destroyed! The thought agonized him, but he followed behind the captain. As the library imploded, the two fugitives cloaked in off-white melted into the masses.

Once at a safe distance, they turned down an empty alleyway and took shelter in its shadows.

"What have you done?" asked the caveman with pain in his eyes. "You've destroyed the greatest library we've ever seen."

"I saved our lives. Those people weren't going to let us out of there."

"But all those books..."

"There's still one left." The captain patted his pouch. "Now let's see that scroll."

"We need to get to the western market. It's for them. Not us."

The captain hesitated.

"Fine," he said flippantly. He pulled out the stolen book and studied its pages.

The caveman, put off by the captain's sudden nonchalance, set out on a mission of his own.

"Where are you going?"

"I'm going to find the western market," the caveman said in defiance.

The captain nodded his head in agreement. "You knew that man, the ghost?"

Tension subsided in the caveman. A look of remorse came over him.

"He was a ghost to me until today." He looked earnestly at the captain. "I don't really understand it. That was the face of my first teacher. I watched him die... a long time ago."

"Maybe we all live and die and live again," the captain quipped with a thoughtful grin.

The captain remained in the shadows while the caveman searched for information. He moved through the strange environment like a man who had been there before. In a sense, he had. There were moments it felt just like his first days in the forest.

The streets grew sparse and quiet. In the absence of crowds, he noticed a graffitied slogan, Free Yedá. He followed its frequency. The deeper he descended into the urban density, the more it appeared.

He was the only person within sight. Turning toward a sky-bridge, he heard the sound of rushing water, and a familiar scent caught his nose. His stomach grumbled as he followed his senses down a long flight of stairs and into an open square full of carts and bodegas.

Strangely, it was barren of life except for three women standing on the manicured banks of an enormous canal. He moved in closer, hiding among the abandoned stalls. The women caught and sold fresh fish.

Unlike those closer to the library, their clothing was colorfully covered in a variety of pastels that seemed to bleed into one another without a pattern. It felt fortuitous.

He decided to make himself known—first catching the eye of the stocky fisherwoman.

“Shouldn’t you be inside?” she asked as he approached.

Unsure of what she meant, but playing along, “Why should I be inside?”

The stocky fisherwoman grinned and said something to the other two in a tongue he couldn't comprehend.

"The city has gone on lockdown in search of two terrorists. Soon, the guard will begin sweeping these streets."

"Then why are you still here?"

"Can we help you?" asked the lanky fisherwoman, changing the subject.

"Well, I'm very hungry and was told I could find some food at the western market. As I'm sure you can tell, I'm not from here. Do you know where that is?"

"This is it, but I'm afraid the options are slim," said the stocky fisherwoman.

"Perhaps you would like to try some fish," said the chubby fisherwoman. "The sandwiches are delicious."

Déjà vu.

This must be a sign, thought the caveman. He opened his cloak, showing the richly hued uniform underneath, and presented the scroll.

Their brows furrowed. More chatter commenced in the unknown tongue amongst them. The stocky fisherwoman studied the caveman and cautiously took the scroll.

Together, the fisherwomen read its contents. They paused. A mysterious excitement filled the air. Their eyes met each other in acknowledging embrace, and then returned to the caveman.

"Where is your companion?" asked the stocky fisherwoman.

The caveman was taken by surprise.

"He's waiting for me back..." he pointed in the direction from which he came.

The fisherwomen sprang into action. The lanky one shuffled around in a bag beneath their cart. The chubby one whispered indecipherable orders into a little, handheld device.

"Good," said the stocky one.

She pulled a box from the canal's rushing waters and set it on the table.

"We must hurry," she said, opening the box.

From inside, she handed the other two women large metal machines the caveman was sure were weapons.

The lanky fisherwoman handed out cloaks just like that which the caveman wore, but in black. The three women disguised themselves, and then handed one to the caveman.

"This is better for lurking in the shadows," said the lanky fisherwoman. Following suit, the caveman switched to black.

The stocky fisherwoman pulled a particularly bright fish from the canal and forced the scroll down its throat. It wiggled furiously but was unharmed as she returned it to the water. It swam away with the current.

"Now, let's go get him," the stocky fisherwoman asserted.

They hurried back to the alleyway, being careful around every corner, to where the captain hid. An unusual quiet gripped the city like the calm before a storm.

Getting nearer, they found themselves no longer alone. The white guard was on patrol, hunting for the captain and the caveman.

"He's just over there," said the caveman, gesturing toward the captain in the distance.

"This way," whispered the stocky fisherwoman.

They went the long way.

The fisherwomen were clever and clearly knew their way around the city. As they approached the captain's location, he appeared from the shadows—dagger in hand.

"Is that you, my friend?" he said, tightly gripping the blade. "Who do you have with you?"

"No time for introductions," said the stocky fisherwoman. "They're closing in."

"Put this on," said the lanky fisherwoman to the captain.

The five black cloaks flowed with the descending night, though it was becoming more difficult to evade the white guard.

The white guard marched through the streets in growing numbers. Under the veil of darkness, the band of rebels averted them until, finally, it was unavoidable. There was only one way out, and a regiment of the white guard stood between them and the gateway.

They huddled.

“What now?” asked the caveman.

“Follow my lead,” said the captain, and without consultation he popped out into the open—the others remained hidden.

“Well, fancy meeting you here,” the captain said, mocking the surprised white guard.

They gripped their weapons.

“Seize him!”

The white guard charged.

Out came the dagger, but the captain did not thrust it into the ground. Instead, he cut his own palm. In doing so, time slowed. The white guard moved like turtles through mud.

“That’s your cue, ladies,” the captain said with his token grin.

The fisherwomen went to work with their destruction machines, shredding the white guard with a barrage of metallic fire.

The caveman looked on in horror as bodies dropped. No matter the justification, he could not stomach it. In series of flashes, the entire regiment was lifeless.

The stocky fisherwoman was unfazed. “More will be coming. Let’s move.”

* * *

They passed through the gateway into a different reality. It was dirty and unpolished.

The caveman saw soil for the first time since arriving in the futuristic place. Trees grew wild and unkempt, unlike the inner city where every piece of green was precisely placed and perfectly pruned.

Most remarkable was the explosion of color that burst in fragments all around. Though it was shrouded in typical shades of white, doors were blue and red.

On every person was an accent of individuality, even if buried in their bleached garments.

Though the vibrancy comforted the caveman, he couldn't tell if they were actually on the ground, or if it was just another level of the man-made metropolis.

The streets buzzed with activity. The caveman felt anxiety emanating from passersby. News of the library's collapse had reached every citizen.

Fear of the looming retribution was heard in their chatter and seen on their faces. Some raised their voices in anger and resistance.

The band in black cloaks wisped through the clamor like a cloud in the night. They turned along another canal and away from the crowds.

The caveman looked up, searching for the guides that were always there, but found none. He could not see the stars, only an overcast mist of darkness. His heart sank.

He wasn't sure chasing the three fisherwomen into the bowels of the unknown was the right thing to do, or if he had any idea what right and wrong were anymore. He lowered his head and kept moving.

Out of the corner of his eye, he saw fish swimming in the canal. One jumped out of the current and hovered in thin air, eventually returning to the stream with ease and grace. The oddity distracted him, and, for a moment, he was engulfed by the wonder of where he was.

They arrived at crossroads of waterways. The fisherwomen leapt into the intersection at full stride. The captain and the caveman followed. There was no splash or sensation of water, only the grip of a current that did not take them along one of the many canals, but downward.

Strangest of all, they could breathe.

"What is this?" the caveman asked of his companions.

No one answered. Maybe no one knew. The captain certainly didn't.

They shot out of the slide and into a room so dim they couldn't see walls or a ceiling. The only light emanated in warm tones from dim, dangling, stained glass lanterns that disappeared into darkness.

The captain and the caveman gathered themselves. The fisherwomen were nowhere to be seen.

Footsteps approached, coming closer and closer. Out of the pitch stepped a woman they both knew well. The captain immediately took a knee for his queen.

There was no mistaking it, she wore a crown upon her head and the royal seal graced her left lapel as it always did, though her dress was no longer that of a monarch, but of a militant.

The caveman rushed to hug her like a lost sister. Laughing, she returned the love, and then made her way to the captain.

He rose, looking deep into her eyes.

She smiled, caressed his cheek and returned his gaze.

They embraced like two halves of a whole separated for far too long.

"You hid from me," she said, confronting him.

He defended himself. "I made a promise. My mission wasn't finished."

"And what about now? Is it finished?"

"It feels never-ending." the caveman chimed in.

The captain chuckled. "That's the most sense you've made yet."

"Alright, we're clear!" the queen shouted into the darkness.

The hanging lanterns multiplied throughout the room in a symmetrical pattern, revealing a circular room covered in tiles. The caveman inspected them.

Each blue ceramic piece was identical and illustrated a yellow triangle with three red eyes. The captain whipped open the stolen book and flipped to a specific page. He showed the caveman. It was an image of the same mosaic wall. On the opposite page was the floor plan and sketch of a castle.

"Welcome to the citadel, gentlemen," the queen said. "Follow me."

She waved her hand over one of the tiles, causing a section of the mosaic to depress into the wall and open, revealing a doorway into a buzzing room of eclectic voices bantering in various dialects.

As the captain and the caveman entered, the occupants of the room hushed and turned their attention to the new arrivals. The caveman noticed that though uniquely dressed, they all wore a sash of red, blue, and yellow—some around their waists, others across their chests.

Limestone walls stretched up to a ceiling of stained glass.

"We've been here before," whispered the caveman to the captain.

The queen introduced them. It seemed as though they were expected. Eager handshakes of camaraderie and excitement greeted them from the collection of new companions.

One in particular emerged with a blue ribbon around her neck—the red medallion unmistakable. She was the same woman from the congress hall. Up close they saw the medallion was etched with the mysterious symbol they had come to identify as Yedá.

"We received the lost page," she said to them. "Thank you."

"The scroll!" exclaimed the caveman, realizing to what she referred, yet clueless as to its significance.

"Yes," said the queen.

"What lost page?" blurted out the ever-inquisitive captain.

The lady with the red medallion pointed to the stolen book still in his hand. "The only one missing from that."

It inspired a second question from the captain.

"And what is that symbol around your neck...and here." He gestured to the same symbol on the stolen book's spine.

The caveman added, "And who or what is Yedá? The man who gave me the scroll told me to ask."

"It is you," said the lady with the red medallion, "and it is me."

Her cryptic explanation went on with a story of epochs passed.

"In the first age, Yedá was representative of the breath that flowed through every living thing, from generation to generation. Evidence suggested the first human civilizations called themselves Yedá, and its meaning was like a form of worship.

"In the second age, one of exponential advancements in the understanding of our natural world and how to harness its power, Yedá evolved from its naive, supernatural interpretation to one that represented the cultivation of a more tangible power. People transitioned from mystics and medicine men to scholars and scientists. They ditched esoteric magic for empirical evidence.

"Humanity thrived, or so it seemed, and by the third age, billions covered the planet. Megacities blossomed. Symbols and their meanings were lost in mathematical laws that governed practical realities. Philosophies of reason and logic overcame the intangible ideas of epochs past.

"Over time, society rejected all things one could not see, smell, touch, taste nor hear. If it couldn't be explained on paper, it was for the foolish. Yet, there were some who saw value in the ancient ways. I come from a long line of those who sought to bring balance between that which we can define and that which we cannot," described the lady with the red medallion. "My ancestors built this citadel at the end of the third age, when Yedá again emerged in the mind's eye of the public."

The lady with the red medallion took the stolen book from the captain. Flipping through for a particular page, she explained the citadel was erected after a visitation by three creatures made of light. She held up the book, showing a picture of an old man.

"My grandfather's grandfather was one of those who experienced this visitation," she said. "There have been many debates and arguments as to the nature of this event. My ancestors swore to its physical reality. Others called it a dream. Nonetheless, the citadel itself became a symbol of the spiritual renaissance that swept the developed world.

"At the dawn of the fourth age, the balance began to break down. Society grew wild and unwieldy. Passions flowed like cheap wine. In the chaos and turmoil, ranks broke, and there emerged a new brand of thought—that knowledge was a dangerous thing.

"The party of white emerged, and in their cunning, they consolidated all human artifacts and antiquity into a singular location. Covertly, they broke down the system of public education. Overtly, they preached a message of censorship and shunned the spirituality that had returned to the cultural zeitgeist.

"As their manufactured influence grew, so, too, did a pious vision of perfection. Skyscrapers grew higher and color vanished from their veneer.

"Once again, Yedá was pushed into the fringes. The citadel was buried in the shiny steel and colorless glass of this new existence. Knowledge became a commodity. The carefully crafted, solitary vault of human history and understanding became increasingly guarded by the party, and information was only leaked upon their blessing. Over time, knowledge of the vault evaporated from common people.

"To the party of white, the vault's contents are only able to be harnessed by those who choose the path of replacing the individual mind with the collective perfection contained in the vault. Ironically, they took their party name from stories of the visitation and the white light they emitted," she scoffed. "But few know those stories anymore. How ignorant we have become."

"The library, that's your vault?" the caveman asked.

"It's much more than a library," said the lady with the red medallion. "The collection of books is only a small part of what's inside the vault. There are sacred tools and instruments, scientific apparatuses, and devices from across the ages. Forgotten magic is held hostage in there."

"But that ends tonight," the queen inserted.

Her comment sparked the room, and the conspirators gathered around a table that featured a series of flames at its center. The fire danced in an unusual way, as if moving in slow motion.

For a moment, the caveman was transported to his experience of drowning. There was no reason, only a sensation exclusive to that borderline. As quickly as it came, he snapped out of it.

The lady with the red medallion placed the stolen book on the table and opened it to where a page had been removed.

The conspirators looked on in suspense, as she revealed the scroll and unraveled it. She set it within the book. The page grew back like a quickly healing wound.

Joy and celebration erupted. Their time had come.

“What does this mean?” asked the captain through the cheers.

“It means we now have a full schematic of this city during the third age, and, therefore, know the alternative way into the vault. We can free it,” said the lady with the red medallion.

Guilt overcame the caveman. “But the vault has been destroyed.”

“No,” replied the lady with the red medallion. “What happened there today is exactly what we needed. The vault was installed in the porous veins of a dead volcano. That lava rock will withstand anything. So, all it has done is shut the party of white out. Now, we’re the only ones with a way in.”

She placed her hand on the book. “Let us pay our respects,” she announced to the conspirators.

They bowed heads in silence, and for a few minutes, not a word was spoken. The altar of peculiar fire danced like a deity—their somber faces tattooed with the oscillating glow of its purpose.

* * *

At the break of day, the conspirators entered the vault. Without fail, the stolen book, complete with its missing page, led them into the extinguished volcano's chamber from underneath.

To their dismay, they were not alone. Within seconds, the white guard descended like an army of insects. The caveman turned with anticipation to the captain, expecting to see him brandish the blade.

He did not.

Instead, the queen stepped forward. She held something. Calmly, she kissed her closed hand and placed it on her chest., The white guard suddenly lost all control, as if blinded. They crashed into the vault walls and cowered from an invisible force—completely incapacitated.

"They must have found a way in from above," said the queen to the lady with the red medallion. "That's our exit. We'll find it. And we'll do our best to take the guard with us. The rest is up to you."

"We will find our own way," replied the lady with the red medallion.

Set on separate purposes, the two said goodbye like soldiers. A nod was all.

"This way," the queen said to the captain and the caveman.

As the guards suffered from the sting of strange magic, the queen and her two most prized knights hurried past them and into another of the volcano's dry veins. They would never again see the lady with the red medallion.

"What did you do to them?" asked the caveman of the queen.

"I scorched their eyes with a light only they can see." She

handed him the small talisman used for that witchcraft. It was a translucent stone engraved with the same symbol at the hilt of the captain's dagger.

"Where did you get this!?" pressed the caveman.

"From an old civilization in the new lands."

Coming down the tunnel from behind, they heard the white guard chasing after them. The spell had worn off. Time ran short. Before the caveman could ask any more questions, the queen abruptly stopped.

"Here it is. Get in!"

Before them was a carriage of some kind.

"I'm driving," said the captain, and they hopped on board.

With a flick of the ignition, the motor rumbled a mechanical growl. As the captain slammed the gas pedal to the floor, the machine came alive.

Shooting through the tunnel at an incredible speed, the white guards were no match for them. The trio ripped through their ranks with ease. The captain curved and cornered through the volcano's corridors as the queen navigated. It was as if she had been there many times before.

They exited the caves into one of the vast columns that extend far overhead. It looked just like the library, but instead of books there were endless unknown treasures. No time for lingering. As soon as they started their assent, gunfire rained upon them. The queen shot back, but the caveman simply dodged the bullets.

"What are you doing?" yelled the queen. "Fire!"

It had been a long time since that bloody day back in the small village. He never wanted to be a part of such murder again. And then a bullet struck him in the shoulder. Pain shot through his body. Shock and anger filled him with adrenaline. In an intoxicating rage, he grabbed his weapon and squeezed the trigger with a beastly cry of battle.

They made it halfway up the column before the white guard assault became too much for the carriage to handle. A tire exploded. The captain whipped the wheel toward the column wall, causing the carriage to flip up onto one side.

It eventually ground to a halt, creating a shelter from the barrage. The battered queen, caveman, and captain barricaded themselves behind the ruins of their chariot.

The queen looked to the caveman. In spite of the onslaught that persisted, her fury subsided in his countenance.

His face was pale and sweaty, and his bloodshot eyes were wide with the terror of war. White knuckles gripped his weapon. His breath was deep and heavy as he turned his gaze upon the captain.

"Why don't you just use your dagger!?"

"It doesn't work like that," the captain yelled back over the machinegun fire pounding around them. "I don't command it. It commands me."

His face pained and tongue tied, the caveman stared back at him with bitter confusion.

"I know it sounds crazy, but it whispers to me, as if an angel on my shoulder," said the captain.

"Or a demon, perhaps," said the queen with regret. She understood the captain's dilemma, for she too heard such whispers.

The caveman let out a sudden sound of anguish as he threw the weapon away and looked down at the hand of his trigger finger. It throbbed with a burning pain. The talisman fell to the ground. He had been holding it whole time, squeezed between his palm and the rifle.

The queen quickly swooped it up, but something bizarre had happened. The symbol, once etched on the translucent stone's surface, was no longer there.

The caveman revealed his hand. Branded upon his palm was the symbol. Somehow it had transferred. Stranger still, the onslaught of bullets stopped and the caveman's fresh wound was healed.

"What does this mean?" the caveman asked.

"I...I don't know..," said the queen, trailing off with a worried tone—her loss of words unusual.

Wind circulated through the column. It rapidly picked up, tossing loose items around them. In the wide vertical cave that spanned from a deep darkness below to a faraway opening of light above, small relics and artifacts were thrust upward. As the wind intensified, so, too, did the devices shooting upward. Wood and ceramic tools became mechanical instruments that grew in size with each item that passed.

As another vehicle flew by, the captain had an idea.

"We've got to jump."

"Yes! And get inside one of those vehicles," the queen said, snapping out of her confusion.

"Exactly," replied the captain.

"I'm with you," the caveman acknowledged.

They fought the winds and stood on the edge. From the depths, a giant metal beast with wings appeared out of the darkness. The queen knew what it was—an airplane.

As it drew near, they leapt into the tornado, grabbed hold of the plane's rudder, and climbed into its interior.

Before he could make it inside, the caveman was struck by debris, causing him to lose his grip and spiral out into the whirlwind. The captain instinctually ripped loose the netting attached to the plane's hull. Firmly holding on to it with one hand, he dove out after the caveman as the queen made her way to the plane's controls.

Upward they flew. The captain swam the squall toward the caveman, who unconsciously tossed in the tempest, out of control. The captain was finally able to reach him.

Once the queen saw the caveman was secured, she whipped the wheel, which yanked the netting, and thrust the captain and the caveman back into the plane.

Once inside, the captain brought the caveman back with a slap, and the two joined the queen in the cockpit.

Up ahead, they saw light beyond the column was fast approaching.

Though disheveled, the caveman felt no fear. To the contrary, joyfulness consumed him. He had been there before. Though he did not know what was on the other side, it was just another cave, and before his eyes just another great light.

The caveman whistled a tune. Calm washed over the queen and the captain, and for an infinite instant they shared a laugh at the absurdity that surrounded them, drenched in the vigor of life.

As they blasted through the opening, the plane lost momentum. The winds stopped, and with it, the force that pushed them upward. Gravity returned.

The caveman heard a strange whisper he couldn't decipher.

As the plane reached its crest before crashing back to the earth, the captain said, "Time to jump ship again."

They threw open the cockpit door and, once again, leapt into the unknown.

Out came the dagger. The captain again cut his hand and held the dagger high. As he did, the three of them were suspended in midair, while everything around them crashed back into the column, disappearing into the darkness.

Relics and artifacts rained around them like a tumbling museum, and they found themselves floating above a courtyard encased in a towering skyscraper of bland concrete and cold steel. Overhead were layer after layer of glass ceilings.

They were gently set back on the ground floor. There, waiting before an open doorway, was the tall man.

"Everything is in place, my queen."

"Good," she said without skipping a beat. "Let's get to the roof."

The caveman was confused. "What is this? What's going on?"

The queen did not answer. She darted through the doorway and into a steel cage. The captain and the tall man did the same.

Once again, the caveman heard a whisper.

"Move like water," it said.

And so, he followed the flow and joined them in the cage.

The door closed, encapsulating them. The tall man punched in a series of numbers on a glowing screen. The caveman was reminded of the submarine. The room moved.

"It's an elevator," the queen said.

"How do you know all of this? And what are we all doing here?" asked the caveman.

As they ascended, the queen explained. "Since you saw me last, I have traveled through time. Those ages you heard of, I've seen them all. I've watched humanity rise and fall and rise once more. In the lab we once dreamed of what stars were like. Well, I've seen us fly to them, only to forget them."

"How is this possible?" asked the caveman.

"There is a fountain of eternal life. When I found it, I believed it key to shaping a world of benevolence and peace. I thought I could end war and eliminate human suffering. It would only take time. But time and time again, I failed."

The elevator accelerated, but the ride was so smooth the passengers remained calmly suspended within its belly.

Like a rocket ship, it shot upward as the queen continued.

"Through the ages, I tried new and different tactics. Emperors and presidents sought my council, while others branded me with villainy. I was both revered and reviled. For a hundred years, I was hunted, unable to jump to another time, as I'd previously done with the aid of the talisman.

"Its mysterious power stopped. Over this dark century, I was eventually forgotten as dictators died and the world became more connected. Technological discoveries diminished the hold of superstition. So, too, did the advancement bury the magic found in the talisman and the dagger. Their glow faded, and the symbol they bore disappeared. I, however, remained ageless."

"Wait...you knew about the dagger?" asked the perplexed caveman.

As they shot higher and higher, the queen went on. She spoke of the next century when she lived mostly in the shadows of world wars and machines of mass destruction. Those eventually gave way to a new century of digital wonder that brought knowledge to people at a rate and capacity beyond anything she had ever seen. It was at the dawn of that century that she saw the captain for the first time since he set sail for the new lands, in what seemed like a thousand lifetimes past.

"Rumblings in the earth disrupted the relative peace," the queen said. "Fires and floods, raging seas, and bitter winters gripped every continent with increasing frequency. In the midst of this turmoil, a plague swept the planet, thrusting the globalized civilization toward chaos and confusion. Digital information poured out from all directions to support every hypothesis and conspiracy. Truth fused with lies. Propaganda prevailed. Biased opinions and petty emotions spun out of control as demagogues emerged into positions of great influence."

"It was like a nightmare," interjected the captain. "I was boarding my ship back home and to my queen. I had just been given the dagger but had not yet unsheathed it. The moment I did, it transported me to this horrid, inundating reality."

The queen returned to her terrible tale.

"I was wandering through wreckage of one of the many riots taking place, searching for answers, feeling as though I did not even know what I knew, when a wild-eyed homeless man approached me."

It was the captain. The queen was overjoyed. For a moment, her loneliness and sorrow dissipated. But she quickly understood the captain was even more lost than she.

"I thought it was a dream until I saw her, and she explained everything to me," said the captain. "At that point, she revealed the dagger that had brought me to this place. Its mysterious symbol was no longer upon the hilt. 'Yedá has become a monster,' she said to me. A tear rolled down her cheek as she placed the dagger in my hands. With those words, the symbol began to show once again. Before I could even process all I had heard and was seeing, she forced my hand to unsheathe the dagger, and instantaneously I was transported back to the ship many centuries prior. Nothing was the same after that. Reality as I knew it had been turned upside-down."

"That was the first time I heard the whisper," confessed the queen. "It told me to let the fire burn. As I pulled the talisman from my pocket and saw the symbol had also returned there, a thought occurred to me: Yedá must die."

Though the caveman did not realize it, the elevator had come to a stop, and the doors had opened behind him.

The queen gestured for him to exit. He did not.

"Wait. What?" rebuked the caveman. "So, this has all been some kind of circus? Some kind of lie? I thought we were here to free Yedá. What do you intend?"

"Walk!" said the captain forcefully, shoving the caveman out the doors and onto a platform, surrounded by a vast, empty space of greyish-blue. He stood upon a thin railing.

Over the edge on both sides was a precipitous drop into the distant city lights below. Above, there were no stars nor sun, only more of the opaque murkiness.

"What's going on here!?" yelled the caveman, shocked by their shift of allegiance.

A menacing resolve boiled in the queen's stare.

"We are going to reignite the fires of this volcano, destroy the vault, and reduce its contents to ash. I thought we might build a new world, but I see now that our time is done. We must be part of this sacrifice. That is, all of us but you." Her eyes indicated the caveman.

The captain darted a look of surprise at the queen. She calmly returned his glance and cocked her head in the direction of the caveman, as if to command the captain.

For a moment, the captain seemed to recoil from his duty. After a few moments he gave in, grabbed the caveman and wrestled him toward the end of the platform.

As the captain and the caveman struggled against one another, the tall man, who had been silent during the assent asked of the queen, "Where is the talisman."

"He is the talisman," she said, referring to the caveman. "Its power has been transferred, but the dagger will suffice."

She turned back to the caveman. "It has been a long time since I have felt hope. But I saw it in your horror of war down below, that deep and humble aversion to violence, and it was verified with the scar on your hand. Be better than us."

She turned and walked with the tall man back into the elevator car.

"Move like water." The caveman heard the whisper again, and he admitted to himself the fight was lost. Finally letting go, the captain threw the caveman from the edge.

He did not fall, however. Instead, he slowly spun in the momentum and floated upward as if in a vacuum.

As the caveman uncontrollably moved away, the captain gave him that familiar smirk, a salute, and then joined the other two in the elevator shaft.

While still in view, the tall man drew a pattern on the queen's and the captain's foreheads. He then cut the cables, and the best friends ever known to the caveman plummeted out of sight, toward their suicidal doom.

There was nothing the caveman could do.

* * *

His body steadily spiraled further from the vaulted platform.

As the futuristic city faded into a blur of lights his spin grew in velocity. He waved his arms and kicked his legs, trying to regain his bearings, but it was no use. In the helpless struggle, rage boiled.

He seethed with anger at the captain, the queen, and the tall man. He hated himself for believing in them, for believing in anything. Even more so, he was disgusted with his capacity for contempt.

Counter to that current, his honest ambition was peace and light. But now, every condemnation was a mirror reflecting his own failure. In his self-loathing, he wailed with agony.

The bluish-grey abyss brightened, as if luminescence poured into the bleak nothing. Still, there was emptiness, and the force of motion made him dizzy and unable to focus.

Hatred became sadness. As consciousness collapsed, the caveman wept. Through his tears, he barely made out a looming shadow. Something was growing, but he could not tell what was up or down.

Closing his eyes, he remembered the submarine and all the moments when he had no idea what was coming for him.

Acceptance washed over like a warm bath.

As best he could, he cracked open his eyes in the nauseating, out-of-control spiral to see the shadow had grown into a giant black hole ready to swallow him.

It did not.

Instead, he collided with a fluffy cloud that gently enveloped him, stopping his spin. As if in slow motion, he bounced off the cloud and over its edge to see tentacles flowing from underneath the blob of its body.

It was no black hole or cloud. It was a giant jellyfish. As he regained full consciousness, he saw the jellyfish were everywhere—thousands of them.

His chest burned, and he realized he'd been holding his breath. It suddenly struck him—he had returned to the sea.

He had a new problem. He couldn't breathe.

As the school of jellies gracefully pulsed past, he vigorously paddled to the closest of them and reached out with his symbol-scarred hand, grabbing hold of a tentacle.

The moment he found grip, he was blinded by a white flash. A jolt of electricity consumed him. Bolts of lightning shot from the jellyfish, through his body, and downward from his feet. As the shocking euphoria overwhelmed the caveman, rumbling was heard in the faraway depths.

When the caveman came to, he was floating on the surface. The sun beamed radiant warmth as he bobbed in the gentle current. He had no idea how long he had been there, or what had transpired with the jellyfish.

Nothing seemed strange anymore.

He adjusted to view the horizon. There was land, and at its center was a perfectly shaped, glacier-crested mountain. The journey went on as he swam for shore.

* * *

An endless stretch of white sand greeted him. It disappeared into a dense juggle, where palms waved in the warm ocean gusts. From within he heard a heartbeat of drums. It seemed to call out, and the repetitive trance beckoned him into the bush and toward the mountain.

As he hiked further inland, the heartbeat grew close. Beneath his feet the earth quaked. In the vibration, he became more aware of his body. Something poked him.

Investigating its origin, he discovered a heavy object nestled securely in his pouch. To his surprise, it was the dagger. He gripped its golden handle and gazed upon the mysterious symbol. He had learned so much and come so far, yet he still found himself lost in the unknown.

He paused in appreciation of the steady rise and fall within his chest. Transfixed in the sublime pulse of his breath and beating heart, time stood still.

His eyes returned to the horizon. The jungle opened up, and before him lay an ancient civilization. It was as though the end of ages from whence he had come now cycled back to the beginning.

Painted people wailed, gyrated, and beat drums as they encircled a blazing bonfire. Night was coming, and the halo of dusk painted a portrait of pastel sky. Two three-sided pyramids framed the triangular mountain that loomed over them all. To one side the sun was setting, to the other the moon was rising. Stars flickered at the peak.

The painted people saw the caveman standing at the edge of the jungle. Their wailing grew louder. Several of them pointed spears and slowly approached him.

Again, the whisper spoke, and the caveman raised the dagger high, one hand on the hilt, the other on the sheath, poised to unleash its unknown wrath.

The painted people froze in shock. The wailing stopped. Drumming ceased.

Through the crowd emerged a chieftain, his head dressed in a plume of feathers. He stood in front of his fellow painted people and opposite the caveman, like two foes preparing to duel.

The chieftain stomped one foot. The caveman felt it in his gifted leg as if he'd done the same, but he had not.

The traumatic memory of losing that leg sent a shockwave down his spine. The ground convulsed and quivered heavier and heavier, like a buried demon trying to escape.

The chieftain raised both hands, mimicking the caveman. The smell of smoke and sound of crackling fire filled the advancing darkness.

The caveman's heart pounded in anticipation. The chief made two fists, and then released. At that same moment, but absent his volition, the caveman unsheathed the blade.

The earth simultaneously burst open at the mountain peak in a tremendous explosion, raining molten rock and ash upon the ancient civilization.

Unfazed, the painted people did not move, and, somehow, the bombs did not strike them. Instead, they chanted a haunting: "Yedá, Yedá, Yedá..."

Over and over they repeated the monotone chorus as fireballs crashed with devastating impact. The pace of their refrain picked up as they parted before the caveman, creating a pathway toward the mountain.

Lava poured from the crater at its zenith. The volcanic eruption continued with blasts so loud it rattled the caveman's chest. His heart beat faster.

He closed his eyes.

Again, he heard the whisper as he took steps toward his apparent destiny.

As he passed the painted people, all heads bowed, and their chant continued. He locked eyes with the chieftain—a towering man who seemed somehow familiar.

Remarkably, none of them were being harmed by the fire that rained from the sky. It was as if they were covered by an invisible barrier that did not allow the catastrophe within their vicinity.

As soon as there was nothing between him and the mountain, the caveman noticed a winding trail to the top. He looked back at the chieftain, who pointed to the peak, and sang a familiar tune. It was the song of the sun.

As the caveman turned back to the mountain, he lifted his voice with the refrain learned in the village long ago. Behind him, the chorus continued, "Yedá, Yedá, Yedá..."

As the caveman began yet another climb, voices of the painted people disappeared into grumblings of the earth and blasts from the volcanic mountain. Intense heat sizzled his skin. Sweat poured down his brow. Yet the golden streams of lava miraculously diverted behind him, making a return impossible, but never encumbering the path forward.

Thick gazes and clouds of floating debris fogged his vision, but his breath was not affected. The smell of smoke filled his nose with pleasure, not discomfort.

Onward he went, again feeling lost in time, for hunger never came and he did not tire.

Wraiths of the past appeared in his transcendent march—trees and forest creatures, fishermen at the banks of the red rivers that flowed through the fog. Onward he walked. The taste of ale and smell of flowers penetrated his senses, transporting him to a time when life was simpler, and all made sense.

One foot after the other he carried on. Sailors and soldiers, knights and revolutionaries waltzed around him in an intoxicating ballet of memory.

Days turned into decades as he ambled up. All the while, the song of the sun surfaced upon his lips. Across the ages, it seemed as though he heard the harmony of faded friends.

The caveman stepped out of the haze that floated below him like a storm cloud. The volcanic activity settled into thundering hum. There were no more explosions. The rivers of lava froze into motionless, black mounds that disappeared downward into the unknown. Out in front of him stretched a ridge with cliffs on both sides. At its end was the mouth of the crater.

He had reached the summit.

The caveman walked along the narrow pathway and noticed a man-made structure at its glowing end. He continued toward it until he saw upon its stone slabs was a beautiful maiden. Her ankles and wrists were chained to what appeared to be an altar.

The unexpected companion pulled him from the daze of his ascendance. A nervous agitation grew in his gut. Drawing near, he felt he knew her.

Regally dressed, she showed no signs of fear, though her demeanor was despondent and her spirit absent.

Moving in, he saw an emblem upon the locks that bound her chains. It was the symbol he had come to know as Yedá. On her forehead was another marking—the gift symbol.

The whisper spoke, but the message changed. Chills rippled across his skin. He remembered the dagger in his grip, its blade calling out to rest in the heart of the maiden before him. He resisted the eerie request but remained compelled.

Remembering the queen's words of necessary sacrifice, he stepped closer to the maiden, wondering as to the fate of his once-beloved queen. He begrudgingly raised the diamond dagger.

Conflict coursed through his conscience. The listless beauty before him made no motion but for her eyes rolling up to the heavens. In them, the caveman found a familiar reflection.

He looked up to see a sea of stars. The same shimmering, far-away mysteries he once branded as lost souls and eventually became his guides on the open ocean. He'd forgotten their spellbinding majesty.

"There is so much yet to discover," he whispered to himself.

Tranquility came over him. He dropped the dagger and walked to the crater's edge. Without hesitation in his gait, he threw himself into the volcano and plunged toward the bubbling, orange brew below.

As the air rushed past, it felt like flying. He peered upon the mountain's inner walls to find an array of dazzling jewels that flickered in the fiery beast's belly.

They gleamed in red, yellow, blue, and every hue, blending together in a palette of perfection. The rainbow of color bounced off the limestone walls and morphed into a universe of mystifying signs orbiting around the caveman. These symbols melted into the stars above.

Looking below, the lava pit was no longer there. Instead the caveman faced three seated figures on a floor of stained glass. They were made of light.

As when they once met, the caveman was no longer a physical presence, but only his consciousness. There was no up or down, no left, right, or in-between beyond the orientation of these bright creatures.

They moved, but rotated in way that revealed another figure behind each of them, and then another behind that, eventually becoming nine vibrant eyes.

Changing direction, they spun. Their speed increased, creating circles from the tracers, and finally became one—a singularity of light.

A familiar euphoria gripped the caveman as his bodiless life force collapsed into the warmth.

He was collected and clean in the commune of eternity.

When he awoke, all was dark except for the white bats that danced around him.

O Captain (Part 2)

There is a darkness covered in light,
A black smile, teeth shimmering white,
Never believed in heaven or hell,
Until I met the devil himself.

Was like a mirror looking into his eyes,
Felt familiar as he pulled me aside,
Said he was a captain, needed a crew,
I took his hand and followed it through.

Sang a sailor's tune,
Riding the waves over the moon,
All the stars seemed to sing 'long too,
Until the ocean went boom.

Our ship was swallowed up,
Bodies scattered as the lightning struck,
Demons from the depth came craving death,
The captain said, "fear ye not",
Jumped overboard and started swimming.

I dove in and stayed on his tail all through the night,
My body aches and my head, it ain't right,
And then he stopped, beckoned me close,
Whispered a secret that nobody knows,
Whispered a secret and sank like a stone.

I float alone, pondering the sun in the morning glow,
Will I stay or will I go?

Release my breath,
Hello, Death,
Come get me, I'm ready,
The truth I'm told, I'll follow.

Good-bye sky,
Won't see you tonight,
New lights, they invite me,
I'll see you again when I open my eyes.

If I don't wake, then you'll know the truth.
Either way you'll know what darkness means to you.

Wily Johnny's Journey to Space

Maybe you wish to write your own story,
Seeking the guts to chase fortune and glory.
Take this wander-filled tale of will and wit,
About a spaceman and his daring sidekick.

Wily Johnny was a jack of all trades,
He'd traveled the world and learned of its ways.
Once summited Everest and sailed the Suez,
In the Bay of Bengal, Johnny saved a princess.

Clever as ever, he sold swimsuits to fish,
Beat Russians at chess and could out-cook the French.
Yes, Johnny was known for all sorts of hijinks,
Legends profess he out-riddled the Sphinx.

Still something weighed heavy on Johnny's wild heart,
His whole life he'd dreamed of a mission to Mars,
But getting to space was a difficult task,
It took him ten years just to perfect the math.

Another decade he spent building a rocket,
The next step was somehow he had to get on it,
He fashioned a capsule and strapped down inside,
Counted 4, 3, 2, 1… then shot into the sky.

Just three days later he slipped past the moon,
It'd be seven months until Mars was in view,
Always prepared, Johnny wouldn't be lonely,
He'd brought along Neptune, the first astronaut puppy.

Though happy they were in the endless expanse,
Neither canine nor human could say what comes next,
Everything's theory in such an adventure,
And Earth's a blue dot in the rear-view mirror.

Never again would they see waves or trees,
They had only each other and a steadfast belief,
That life wasn't lived from the comfort of home,
We are meant to explore and expand what is known.

Thus, onward they flew to the planet of red,
They ate peanut butter, freeze-dried berries, and bread,
Took vitamins, supplements—all that bodies need,
Each day they played fetch in zero gravity.

Memorized constellations, made up silly games,
Did yoga to keep from going insane,
Day after day, tumbling into the dark,
Ran test calculations to stay on the mark.

All went exactly as Johnny designed,
That's until he realized he'd lost track of time,
This wasn't due to a lack of attention,
Devices act strangely in this new dimension.

Much to Neptune's and Johnny's surprise,
The rings of Saturn now filled their eyes,
Mars and Jupiter surely passed in their sleep,
And somehow, they skipped asteroid belts in-between.

Now, they had a big problem to solve,
The air in the capsule would soon be all gone,
No going back, Johnny made a new plan,
He picked Saturn's moon as a new place to land.

They had to work quick and shift the momentum,
Neptune rearranged the rudder, Johnny shut down the engine.
Like lightning bolts both of them ran toward the back,
Ignited their jetpacks and opened the hatch.

Into the vacuum of space with a blast,
A cable in tow they were tied to the mast.
It created a force that caught solar winds,
Whipped the vessel toward Saturn and began quick descent.

Climbing back in the capsule, they bent into orbit,
Johnny turned on the thrusters, pup the landing gear sorted.
They buckled up tight as the atmosphere grew,
What lay down below neither one of them knew.

Blinded in the midst of dark, misty clouds,
Johnny trusted his instruments to guide them to ground.
With a thud they landed on Titan's Mount Doom,
Green fumes all around in a sea of sand dunes.

They peered out of the ship to rainbow barrage,
Rain fell like cotton crystals in this land of the gods,
Odd though it was, the terrain wasn't hostile,
They geared up to go, and then stepped from the capsule.

Another leap for mankind, he radioed back,
For animals, too, Neptune's due respect,
Into the sunrise, the two carried on,
For answers awaited upon the horizon.

What happened after is never quite clear,
But it's worth a ponder next time you feel fear,
Think of wily Johnny and his furry best friend,
It takes lots of courage to get to the end.

About the Author

Michael Dustin Youree is an American artist originally from Dallas, Texas. Following graduation from the University of Colorado in Boulder, he moved to New York City where he worked in film and music production, taught private music students, and maintained an extensive schedule of performance and philanthropy.

While traveling and touring extensively throughout the Americas, Europe, Oceania, and Asia, he produced a significant portfolio of travel films, short stories, photography, and songs.

Ballads and Bedtime Stories is his first book. You can find his other volumes of work, get to know him, and contact him at *www.mdy.world*.

www.ingramcontent.com/pod-product-compliance
Lightning Source LLC
Chambersburg PA
CBHW080810020826
48982CB00018B/1016

9781938505546